SIX NIGHTS A WEEK

SIX NIGHTS
A WEEK

EVELYN HAWES

HARCOURT BRACE JOVANOVICH, INC.
NEW YORK

First edition

ISBN 0–15–182740–0

Library of Congress Catalog Card Number: 78-160403

Printed in the United States of America

A B C D E

TO NAT HAWES

SIX NIGHTS A WEEK

1

How ever did it happen? I don't like to shop; much prefer to wear my uncle's raccoon coat, instep length, salvaged by me from the moths in the attic. Imagine my surprise when I found myself selling short shorts to half sizes. I even developed a pitch, carnival style, for the retail business. Oh, the retail business; "Madam, may I help?" Widen the eyes, sway—"Sir, she'll love it. I promise." Promises are made to be broken, but not by me. I promise.

How ever *did* it happen?

This is how.

When the buzzer sounded in my room, I'd given my usual leap. I thought of sending a message that I'd left for San Jose, the ploy used when we were unavailable. But that's a coward's way out of a no-see date, especially one that has been on the grill for six weeks. I brushed my hair twenty times because I was twenty and had a fetish about it. I said, "Rapunzel, Rapunzel, let down your hair." See, hers was twenty ells long. When I was a sprout my mod mother forbade fairy tales for fear of upsetting me. Naturally I went to the library and read every one; gave me

3

nightmares, all right. One thing, after *Hansel and Gretel,* I stayed away from ovens.

The buzzer gave off again. I fought an impulse to arrive sliding on the banister. Good thing. Mac doesn't go for planned cuteness, I found out later; probably because he finished college and is part of the world, and older. Also, he hates a put-on.

Stafford Macfarlane. The kind of hunk I like, complete with humorous mouth and tough eyes. Prove-it eyes; not mean, not broody. Direct. Gray. Black lashes. I have heard gray-eyed people are cold. Not so. Take my word.

The university life had, frankly, begun to bore me. Men who had a goal other than kittens were in the libe or lab or class; they didn't seem to be where I was. I had closed the door on the drug scene in high school, so there was no chance of a daze with a mind-buster. The political types sought females who could recite a party line, frequently Mao's, plus constant applause—Big You, Little Me. To them, sex was an hors d'oeuvre (disguised in various ways, as hors d'oeuvres usually are) to the main course of maneuvering the masses. Ape. I am not recreation, or a sex symbol, or a mass.

Winter quarter, junior year, I wasn't with it, so I got a job as waitress in The Gasthaus in the mountains. Ski. *Wunderbar?* Not really, because I doubted my mostest would ever come off the slope and condescend. The future Olympic super-ski jocks didn't have time, and the others were cop-outs, like me. I had thought I was tired of studying, and I convinced my parents I was tired, had gone through school too young and too fast. I didn't need their permission to goof off, of course, but they're great types, and care. So do I. We agreed I had an identity crisis.

My father said, "All right. Yours is a generation that uses

4

words for weapons, and half the time you don't know what you're shooting. But if you're exhausted, stop."

I stopped.

I found out what tired meant, waiting tables and being nice to tourists for tips. My feet hurt all the way to my neck, and above that my ears echoed with grunts and slurps. Also, there wasn't much time to ski; I was not paid for that. Around the fire, late, we talked about being involved, and we were. With ourselves. It was fun and nowhere and as juvenile as Rapunzel. At The Gasthaus, I saw the value of an education. Registered at the U. spring quarter, went to summer school, and was back in the same old drill, senior year. Nothing lost except Shangri-la that never was.

Meeting Stafford Macfarlane, I went ooph for the first time since eighth grade and *he* hadn't known I was alive. Mac noticed immediately. He said afterwards that his eyes lit up because he ate shaped blonde; breakfast, lunch, and dinner. For snacks, he liked tawny-eyed blonde. (I have rather a monotonous color scheme.) When I look back, the statement about appetite is significant, because lovers do try to consume each other.

There are some very indigestible bits.

We went out to Mac's wheels, a senile M.G., and charged off to the Cheese Factory. People were tasting cheese that fall. The Factory had every kind under the sun, and some varieties that had molded sunless. I refused even to try the stuff with the green strings that reminded me of underneath Mrs. Kildane's house the time I got trapped. Tige, our dog, had pursued a skunk and was stuck. I crawled under to help. He went out the way he came in, and I was alone with mildew and skunk. Dad says Tige is the best of all breeds, and he inherited the survival instinct from every mix in the ancestry. You wouldn't believe how much that dog has survived.

So Mac likes cheese. When he kissed me good night, he smelled like a triple cross of goat, yak, and camel cud. Since I had confined my tasting to the rat stuff Mother uses for unwary mice, his good-by tuned me out. But not permanently.

From that moment on, I was not rational. He wasn't, either. We were not suited, and that was almost the only thing we agreed about. I had always sworn a tremendous swear that I would never, never be a part of the crass business world, and Mac *was*.

Ever since the computer had a breakdown freshman year and missed a name and I received someone's grade that was even more realistic than mine, I have not trusted computers. Statistics leave me cold. I dropped the stat course while I could still count on my fingers. And when I see a round haircut (I equate computers, statistics, and round haircuts; they seem to be part of the business world), I have re-entry problems. Mac doesn't have a round haircut, his is British thick—casual hirsute, a modest, non-vocal put-down of the Establishment.

Actually, Mac has no quarrel with the Establishment, which he defines as anyone who has more money and/or a better job than he does.

Business majors and English majors should never meet. They don't, very often; they are rarely in the same area, politically or physically. The humanities (English, soc., etc.) are left of center, near or far, usually, and science and business have a tendency to be right of center, although not always. Of course, no one knows where center is. Everyone talks, but radicals and conservatives don't communicate. A student who tries to find the middle road may flounder and bog down, *sans* teeth.

6

"The name of the slough was Despond," said John Bunyan.

Moderation is not in.

We live in a state of mind. Milton pointed out that mind can make a heaven of hell, and a hell of heaven. The generation gap is nothing compared with the philosophy gap. Some older people alarm me, but no more than the college sophomore, who can be more terrifying than the Lord of the Flies.

I enjoy talking with my parents, although they do have a tendency to huff and puff.

"Peace movements," says my father. "I was there. Never another war; we would not tolerate it. Your mother was with me; we met at a meeting. Decency unto others. Peace, Brother. That was in 1937, Katie."

I marveled. "I wasn't even born."

"We weren't married," Mother said. "Not until 1940. No money."

"Marriage licenses cost," said Dad. "You're not the first generation to consider the future and how it ought to be. We worked for higher wages and people's rights and housing and children's welfare. We won, sometimes."

"When Eric started school, I was active in the PTA," said Mother. "Funny-funny to the Yips, I suppose. Well, that's one way of caring about children. I joined an improvement club; we were interested in improving the library and the streets and everything else. You know what, Katie? Young marrieds don't seem to want to volunteer for an improvement club, now. Mundane. Rather march than do the gut work. I think the country is grinding to a holocaust halt."

"That's not fair," I said. "So what happened to your peace movement?"

"Pearl Harbor," said Father. "I drew the South Pacific,

and then Germany. Infantry; more jungle-crawling and trench-inching than walking. Stopped off in the U.S. on my way to Germany. Eric was born while I was in Europe."

"I began to wonder if your father ever existed." Mother smiled. "But I had certain proof."

"I wondered if I would continue to exist," Dad said.

I nodded. "Yes, and we've been all through this."

"Listen, Katie . . . listen?"

Sometimes I called my father "Father"; sometimes I called him "Dad." Now he was Father. But I want to make it clear I have a lot of respect for him, and for my mother.

At that moment, my parents were several worlds apart, remembering. Mother worked in a factory, lived with her parents; her mother looked after Eric. Dad went from here to there, and back, and over there. My mother was waiting and hoping and standing in line for bacon and gasoline, and my father was in the action, moving on. They were so different. Even their memories were not the same.

There is an odd affinity between opposites: musicians and mathematicians; brown eyes and blue eyes. And why is it that people who stay late at parties develop an urge for people who want to go home early? There are many more examples of this sort of thing.

Mac and I were typical. I knew at once he would not tolerate artsy-craftsy, which I tend to be. I also think it is interesting to rap about how everything ought to be changed before it is too late. Mac does not. He is against war, poverty, pollution, and racism.

"Conversation becomes repetitious," says Mac. "Let's live it."

He does not care to review his experiences in Vietnam, and he doesn't like yackety-yuk about anything. Yet he's

8

not exactly silent, either. "The university is a prelude," he said once. "Kindergarten to life. The profs are ivory tower, and the students precocious—on the brat side."

Made me furious.

He could be articulate, all right, but ordinarily went ahead and did what had to be done, in his own way.

We were in orbit, Katie Rogers and Stafford Samuel Macfarlane. The idea of mate date is getting to know one another. We never did. Went around in a coma. This can be entertaining when it is not driving you out of your skull.

We found that we had to watch *out,* which may have been a step forward.

Winter quarter, Joanie moved in with her man. Left the dorm. It wasn't my business, and I don't judge, except for myself. I guessed whatever they had going was plus.

Mac said, "Stone age."

"They're responsible and committed. I don't see what difference a ceremony makes."

"Sometimes it doesn't." He agreed with me. "You want to share the bag this weekend?"

He was going on a three-day walking trip on the peninsula with the Mountaineers. Sleeping out.

"No, I don't." I was brusque.

He laughed.

"When two people care. . . ."

"We do. You special?"

"What do you think?"

"Why, yes, you are special." He settled the question.

We had made ground rules. As Mac pointed out, it would be great if we could avoid making fools of ourselves. We didn't want to use each other, either. We'd wait for marriage before we opted bed and board. Marriage is still a going concern—check the statistics. All the talk about universal sex strikes me as funny. It's universal, all right.

Joanie made her decision. I made mine.

"Sweet Kate," said Mac. "You having a brain wave?"

I threw a book at him; he caught it.

Thinking, I said, "I don't want to be part of the system, any system. When I was a freshman, gung ho, I joined the group. Took me a while to find the professor we marched for was a freap, and I was his tin soldier. Came to me, a little late, I didn't like the issue, either. I began to wonder how the group got to be so godlike. I only hope that never, never, never again will I act in concert. I'll think for myself."

"So?"

"So I believe in the individual."

"Good way to lose," said Mac.

"All right. I lose. Depending on the angle, there isn't much difference between a group and a mob."

Mac shrugged. "You can overdo the individualism, too. My aunt does. At her house the table is always set."

"What?"

"Table is *set*. Between meals, and all the time. Sour milk. She doesn't like to pick up or wash dishes, so she doesn't. Egg on the fork. Same way about laundry; doesn't go for washing. Stiff socks."

"Can it be you'd rather have a housekeeper than a wife?"

"When we're married you'll be working part time, and writing. We live dirty?"

I had always concentrated on composition. "We'll be partners."

"Keep my hours in mind?"

"Yuh. You do the same for me."

He reached for me. Yuh!

We knew we'd have to share, but we never guessed how gruesome the word *share* would become. Basically, share involves duty and fairness and kindness. If I didn't appreciate those things when applied to *me*, I'd throw up.

When I considered coolly (away from Mac), I knew it was best for me to graduate from the university before we married. If there's too much going on around me, I fog.

By spring quarter that senior year, we got down to the facts of life: eating and rent and stuff like that. Sex is easy, but an apartment is hard to find. If you don't pay the gas bill, you've got no heat. Man, it's cold outside.

We had our year of flipping, and it was golden—with the exception of the episodes. After one episode Mac said he would build a windmill for me. I enjoyed his literary allusion; he didn't make many. I preferred, however, not to be reminded.

We were at a football game because Mac wanted to go. We balanced sports with concerts; one for him, one for me. Sitting beside us at the game was an old man, forty or fifty at least, with friends. They were drinking out of a flask, all very F. Scott Fitzgerald, 1926. The clown next to me drank too much. He got his foot caught between the bleacher stringers, and couldn't pull it out. Those disgusting middle-aged jerks left him helpless. They walked out on a friend before the game was over. Rotten. Well, this little leaguer was groaning and twisting. I did what I could. Took his shoe off (someone must have cared; no stiff socks), and we were home free, but then his foot went limber, and I couldn't put the oxford back on. While I was trying, he gave a giant hiccup and hit me on the back and yelled, "You sure did it, Shishter!"

The game was over; the gun went bang, and I dropped

the shoe. There it was, twenty feet below. The two of us peered down into the murk.

Mac had nearly got to the ground in a series of giant leaps. We always left in a hurry because of the traffic problem. I called to him and he went underneath the seats, rescued the footgear. Tossed it up to me.

Just then a university patrolman came along. "What's the trouble?"

That poopin' drunk stood up and pointed dramatically at Mac. "He shtole my shoe." He added, "Shoe th' ole hosh, shoe th' ole mare, . . ." and fell back.

Mac emerged from the depths, brushed the soot and cobwebs from his new suède coat, and told the patrolman the facts.

On the way to the dorm we were quiet. Mac didn't naggle, but he sighed frequently.

I said, "One can't ignore a stuck foot."

"No."

"One has to help people."

"Yes."

"When someone is in trouble, you can't leave it up to someone else to help."

"True."

So I have a tendency to tilt at windmills. Mac is no Sancho; he is not going along for the ride, and he would never wear a bowl for a hat. To Mac, a bowl is a bowl, not headgear.

In the heat of an argument, I point out that one has to think empirically.

Mac says, Now, just what in hell is that?

It is a good idea, that's what.

There were other rifts. One evening we were in the TV room waiting for doubles, Ken and Linda, before going for coffee. I guess I began it by saying there was no place for the liberal-arts type, like me, in business.

Mac replied there was. Creative imagination was always respected.

Carried away, I suggested he would be happier if he quit working for a retail chain.

"Name is Macfarlane," he said. "Ancestors came over from Scotland. Buy and trade and sell. Hudson's Bay. There's nothing more exciting than the retail business. There is no better company than the J. C. Penney Company."

SOUND BUGLES! CHARGE!

Right then I should have stopped flapping, but I didn't.

"Sure, it's great and coast-to-coast, and I buy that. But what's so wonderful about selling handkerchiefs?"

I didn't realize a Scottish temper is a force of nature, and that aggravating it is like tickling a typhoon. At the time, I wasn't even aware Mac was *in* a temper.

"Have you ever thought what would happen if we all went bummer? Could wear bearskins, if there were any bears left. Squirrel is more like it. Everyone in the world would have knee-length whiskers. . . ."

"Actually, only about half the population," I said. "Kindly tell me what is wrong with a beard?"

"Nothing. Sure, my grandfather had one. *I* grew one. It was hot, it itched, and one drop of strawberry jam and I had to wash the thing; a coffee dribble, and you're an untouchable. I am stating that as far as I am concerned, practically speaking, beards are for the birds. Mine," he added, "was red."

"You must have resembled the auburn-mustachioed Vandyke *Fledermaus*."

He totally lost his temper. "Make a law forbidding the

electric shaver," he snarled. "Forget about my right to think as I please. The hell with sanitation. Pluck your eyebrows with a damned clamshell. . . ."

"Why damn the clam?" I asked clamly—I mean calmly. "Anyway, I do not pluck my eyebrows."

"The way things are with you intellectuals"—he spoiled the effect here, because he is fairly intellectual himself— "we ought to quit. When boobs like me walk out, you think it will be a better world? I'm the man at the hand-kerchief counter, am I? Without me you couldn't keep your nose clean."

"Shocking," I murmured, the way the British do.

We were childish. We knew it; we couldn't help it.

He was off. Out. "Everything is manufactured or grown or made. Medicine and materials and wheat. Food. Every-thing you wear and most of what you eat. Have you been weaving lately? Raised a potato? Compounded a cure? Guys like me grow it and make it, develop it and sell it. Bungs and bung holes."

"Fascinating. Bungs. Who wants one?"

He jumped up and put on his coat, buttoning it fast.

"You've got the wrong bung in the hole," I pointed out mildly.

He blew. Ripped off his coat, buttons popping. "Now you hear this. . . ."

"Keep your voice down," I said, raising mine. "Maybe we're *all* needed. Writing is important; it's life plus in-sight."

He entered the quiet phase, more dangerous than the noisy one. "Life. Sure. The bull business. Thank you."

"For what?"

"For not saying 'Tell it like it is.' "

"What a quaint expression. No one uses it any more. But I'll say what I like the way I want to. Okay?"

14

He laughed. "Linguistically, you reach. They used to tell us in comp the idea was to make yourself clear. Not any more. Cloud the issue and be a genius. Add the gutter words."

"Too common."

"How about your friends?"

"Guilt by association. What is close to the gutter?"

"So an addict calls heroin 'smack.' Speak like an addict, man. Call it 'smack.' Inspiring. May I say 'It's a gas'?"

"It is, indeed. Language is ever changing. And man, we don't much say 'man' any more. Dated, y' know?"

"The same old ideas are still around, under new names. We never catch on."

"You should join a commune, Mac. Might pick up something."

"Yeh, just about anything. When I got out of the army, I tried that. New Mexico. California. The first was the army all over again—plans, duties, How To Avoid Both. The other was so loose it was chaos, and everyone spun out. There's another word for what we were trying to do. It's co-op farming." He shook his head. "*Farming*. None of us had the experience or guts to make it. A great scene. When they started borrowing gas and motorcycles from the town civic center, I got out before someone shot off my ears and other parts."

"So you didn't like to farm. You putting it down, dude?"

"I didn't have it. I didn't like it. It's down for me. Actually, we were sad. We were trying, like Thoreau. He didn't like farming, either."

"Sad. Yes. Thoreau made some points, though."

"Sure. Now, Katie, you teach from a book. Do you write the text from your empirical experience? Who prints those texts the so-called experts throw together? What does it take to make an expert? At least in the retail business we don't pretend to be what we are not."

"How about those jeans that fell apart? Let the buyer beware?"

He gritted his teeth. "You did *not* get the jeans at Penneys."

He was right.

"Anyway, business certainly has a responsibility for whatever *is*."

He picked up his coat, refraining from putting it on, because of the bungs, I suppose, and left. Slammed the door.

When Ken and Linda arrived, I told them we'd split and went to my room. By the time Mac called, days later, I had resigned myself to joining the Corps for Incorrigibles. We had a conversation. We agreed we would give due consideration to each other.

Common courtesy.

So we were going to be radioactive again. Mac said he'd be over.

Whenever I thought of marriage, I would remember my cooking, which was nonexistent except for chocolate pudding. (Seven days a week, chocolate pudding?) I also wondered about finding a place to live, and worrying about these things drove me up the wall. They say the first year of marriage is crucial. It is crucial before the first year.

By the time Mac arrived at my room, I had pushed everything lying around loose under the bed. Our rooms in the dorms are living rooms. I consider it a silly idea, because I don't pick up after myself all the time, and I have a right to be a slob when no one is around. I like privacy, too, and there isn't much. I need peace and quiet. When you have a freak roommate with freak friends, you find layers and layers of personality people lying around your room, picking their toes. I voted against men and visitors in the dorm, and lost.

After I began to think of the dorm as a boardinghouse, I settled down. Except for exhibitionists, we dressed to go into the hall. Contrary to what parents think, co-ed dormitories and relaxed visiting rules probably de-emphasize the biological urge, although I would like to have been protected at times. One thing: I never cared for strange guys with moss on their teeth and mucus in the corners of their eyes. Early-morning stuff. They must have felt ditto.

The concept of marriage, including moss, bothered me more than a boardinghouse, but no other plan appealed to me, either. Running naked in the breezes, à la the flicks (those people must have more red corpuscles than I do), pursued by an equally bare and panting satyr (either sagging or spaced out) strikes me as hilarious, especially when you give some thought to the inevitable goose-pimples, hay with thistles, and/or rocks in the sand. Bed scenes are phony when you remember the camera crew and consider the audience voyeurs. Add to these factors the kind of grief that comes from being worked over and passed around, and it's thumbs down. According to the educational films, epidemic VD is worse than the measles. Much. I hated the measles.

We think differently from the older generation.

I said to my mother once, "To us, sex is not fun and games, and neither is it pure romance; could be we're more idealistic than you senior citizens."

Mother said, "Possibly. Life tends to make us cynical."

I took a poll of my floor at the dorm. "What's a good date?"

There were those who voted for bed activity, but most plumped for a beach fire at night in the summer, and roasting hot dogs and marshmallows; finding sea shells, digging clams. The transistor on, dancing on the sand (no rocks) under the canopy of a star-strewn, fake-fur sky. A walk in the rain; holding hands with your man; kissing. Hot chocolate at Charlie's. A study date at the libe, with the right one. Or the ski slopes on a good day, and mulled wine and candlelight in the evening.

A little mystery. While we're young.

We don't want so much, and what we want, we don't have.

It was surprising, that poll. I mean, girls with everything going for them and girls with nothing going for them voted the same: no pad, no pot, no grabs.

I never made the results public. Who would have believed? Then a research team from Stanford reported much the same for the now scene. It was a relief to find I was not crazy.

So Mac came over.

We settled down.

"It's just that Shakespeare said it all, Mac. We have to be different." I wanted him to understand.

"How many ways can you say whatever you have to say, Katie? Take a business letter; it's exact."

I could feel my lips tighten. "Oh? I thought very little reading was done in business?" Why did I *do* this? I knew the road signs but couldn't stop.

"We read for information, for new ideas. We have to have enough experience to know what is new."

He wanted *me* to understand.

"Some of the thoughts you art students dredge up were

rejected by the ancient Greeks during the great period, before they went down the drain."

"All right. All right," I muttered drearily. "What'll we do with the jerks?"

"I can tell you one thing. The boss isn't going to go for another way of throwing a brick; he'll try to build with one."

I can't stand to be talked to like that.

All holy.

Neither can Mac.

We both blew. He stormed out, and I followed him down the hallway, speaking in low, vicious tones. It was serious.

It is terrible to cry in the early spring, when the buds are budding. I mean, a person ought to be happy with another chance, which is what spring is. This year, you think, maybe there won't be blight or leaf mold or bugs. I sang my own song. "No bugs this spring, tra-la-la tawoo-witta-woo; sing tiddley, sing tiddley. . . ."

Lonely. Oh, lonely.

During the two-and-one-half-week break, I cried a lot. In spite of our disagreements, partly because of them, Mac was the one for me. He was real.

Then I saw Mac's aunt at the Quad, the one whose table is always set. She is a darling and very Auntie Mame. I waved away the smoke from her filtered cigarette in the filtered cigarette holder (she has more than a modicum of caution), and we sat on one of the cold stone benches.

I waved at her smog again. Why will they do it?

She laughed. "What's *your* hangup?"

To my horror, I said, "Mac." I burst into tears. "I'm wild for him."

Basically it was a tactical error, and no one has ever forgotten it. Auntie told Mac I truly loved him. She may have exaggerated, although I am not sure that is possible. Anyway, he called again.

I guess we had learned something.

I used to imagine that when I fell in love there'd be understanding, but I suppose what I hoped for was agreement. It is not possible for two people to agree on everything. It would be ghastly to live with someone who goes up and away as often as I do, and I know it. I need ballast. Could be Mac needs to let loose some grit, occasionally, and float. Perhaps subconsciously we knew these things. We all look for tenderness, but we don't often give it and rarely receive it . . . but between us, there *was* tenderness.

To my family and friends, even to Mac, I pretended I had no doubts about our future. I did, though. Often in the night, I'd take fright and consider running away. In the daytime, I had more sense.

I worried about the way Mac talked of "the boss." In the unpredictable future, would he be the boss? Would he fire people, or be fired from the job? I know there has to be some kind of order, and I'd read about monkeys—who alarm me because we're so close. Well, if there is no leader in a community of monkeys, they become so frustrated that they indulge in gang warfare. They fight, choke, bite, and drown one another whenever possible. Maybe there has to be some kind of a boss? Who's it going to be? Home-grown dictators are no answer; kings are passé. Guess we've got to try to keep each other in line, and that's what we're doing. I think.

But I wondered where all this freedom I'd heard about *was*.

The summer I bicycled through Europe, I didn't find freedom. By September, in fact, whenever I saw men and women (usually women, God Help Me) hoeing the fields or loading manure or sweeping the street (naturally I was not traveling with the jet set), I said my prayers and located my passport. I developed castle fatigue and museum madness, but I didn't run across freedom in the European version. The people were ultimate, mostly, but then people are, mostly.

Or are they? People seem to be the main trouble with the world.

That's the kind of thought Mac puts into the circular file.

By the end of my senior year, Mac and I had met each other's parents, liking both sets rather more than we expected. Mac had a typical male reaction; he was suspicious of my father, who heartily reciprocated.

Mac thought that while he was lucky (which is what my parents believed), I was lucky, too. This was an area both of us felt would not support discussion.

As far as I know, Mac's parents had no qualms. I was their son's choice, period. I had heard that men's mothers could be difficult. Mrs. Macfarlane was wonderful to me. Probably she had been ground smooth by her husband's Scottish granite.

That was a thought-quake.

I had a session with Father and Mother during spring vacation. Mac and I had decided he need not ask for my hand in marriage; to each his own.

Father said, "You are too young to marry."

"I am now twenty-one. Ancient. How old should I be for matrimony?"

Father said, "Thirty."

We all realized: ridiculous.

Father insisted I lived on cloud thirty-seven. Maybe I was looking for an escape?

"There is no escape, Katie. Before I was sent to the European theater, I was in the South Pacific. You've heard of Bali Hai? Even then, in the Dark Ages," he grinned, "it wasn't what it was cracked up to be. You didn't just lie under a breadfruit tree, waited upon by beautiful handmaidens. There were few handmaidens and a large number of insects. Insects have to eat, so they ate everything, including me. They were also interesting parasites; that is, interesting to those who did not have any. You have to live in this world. It's all we have."

"Mac is my world." I meant it.

"Katie, we can't help you," said Mother.

My father owns a hardware store in a small town, and Mac's father is retired. The Macfarlanes go to the city only when there are specials at the supermarkets. They buy the two-cents-less-a-can brands.

My mother went on. "There will be no checks from home and little good will from mankind, in case you are thinking of exploring the reason for *being*. I understand there are young people who do, meanwhile knocking off Laundramats and pay telephones for extras on the theory that you can't rob a *machine*."

She shocked me. She was up on the scene, all right, but the one she described was not ours. I told her so. "Mac works. He works for the J. C. Penney Company. You should hear what he thinks about the destroyers."

Mother apologized in distracted fashion.

I made my voice light and careless. "Well, so we have decided. After proper family conference."

Father closed his eyes. "You haven't any friends in the city."

My heart ached because they cared so much, so terribly. And they were old.

"We have each other."

Hopelessly, my father said to Mother, "Katie is a dreamer. She always was." He looked at me. "Going to fix everything up for everyone. I remember when we took you to see *Peter Pan*—you were seven—and on stage Wendy wondered who she was, and you stood right up and shouted, 'Don't worry, Wendy, I know who I am. Katie Rogers! You can come to live at our house.'"

I remembered, and chose to forget it. Whenever I go to a play, I identify. I concentrate so hard reading a book that I once ate a dime thinking it was the gumdrop that was in the *other* hand. It's awful. During a sad, sad flick it doesn't do any good to tell me it isn't happening. I suffer. I weep. Worst of all, now I'm not so sure who I am, or what. Sometimes I don't even feel human. And sometimes I'm not proud of being human when I am.

Anyway, I don't want to hear about how I used to be, or how my parents used to be, either. The time is now.

Mother said, "All right, Katie. If you are determined to take this step, well and good. No running to Daddy and Mother with complaints. When you marry, that's it. You understand?"

For someone so soft, Mother can be diamond hard. It might have been in the back of my mind that if Mac and I had a serious rumble I could pack my bags and move home. Mentally, I unpacked. Mother meant it. She always did when she said "well and good."

"I'm in love."

Mother looked at me. "Yes."

Dad said, softly, "Keep in mind, Katie, 'Love is not love which alters when it alteration finds.'"

Shakespeare. Well. I mean . . . see, I didn't know my father had read the Sonnets.

Daddy and Mother capitulated. It wasn't that they didn't like Mac or believe in him. They were afraid. My parents would have felt better if Mac and I had had a reserve, financially. They didn't want me to be an old man's darling, but they would've liked my future to be a vista of serenity.

You know those turn-of-the-century paintings? My grand-mother had one. When I was small and visited her, I used to sit with a glass of milk on the blue plush chair, legs sticking straight out, and lose myself in the picture. There was a wide path into a grove of trees and Roman columns in the background. Blue skies, fluffy clouds. The grass was Paris green. Actually, living there would probably be poisonous; too easy. Storms strengthen the roots, but I don't like storms, and I couldn't care less about roots. I'd never been in the rough weather my parents had experienced. I knew it.

Father and Mother told me often enough I had inherited a better world than they did, what with the Depression, a total war, Korea, and what not. Could be. But that is just the point; we hope to avoid their thing. I realized, though, that whenever I'd been cold and shivering and wet through, there had always been a short walk to shelter. That's why my parents worried about my future. I did, too, but not as much.

There was another factor in their concern, which we did not mention.

They wanted everything right for me, and there were no guarantees. There never are any. My brother's death had almost destroyed us; it was frightening that he could die. If anyone should be alive, Eric should. I don't know how to tell about it. Mac advises plain statements. Without the agony. All right. My brother was considerably older than I was; we liked each other very much; we laughed a lot. Eric was big for his age, always; and at seventeen he was everything: All-State basketball player; tops in studies. Scholarship stuff. And going to take premed, then medicine. Pediatrics. He was the original Pied Piper. Every child in town followed him—the stupid ones, the reasonable kids, and the little monsters. He loved them, honestly he did. They knew it. And when he was a physician, he would see that they all had a chance. A chance. But Eric didn't have one. He was climbing Big Knob, the mountain near town, with some other boys, and he fell. He was within reach of the top of the highest cliff and he fell and he died, all broken.

So much promise, so many gifts. Gone. Far away, my brother. Eric. Never, never again laughing.

Like that. Never again.

I was not science-minded. Lab courses were not for me, but I thought and thought about what I could do in memory of Eric, in my fashion. I wanted to stroke for him. I would, I thought.

It was agreed Mac and I would be married in June. Mother said she'd call the church and settle the date, and I requested some small changes in the service. There would be no bridal showers. Father said he appreciated business at the store, but was not bucking for it.

There was a lot to consider.

Tradition was the word. I'd be a June bride. I wasn't going to stand on a hilltop, spring breezes tugging at my simple shift (torn jeans? midi-maxi-micro?). I wasn't going to kneel in an amber field of grain, holding the hand of my brawny (lanky) one, and Come To An Understanding. I am not mocking the hilltop; in a way, it was what I preferred.

What I was going to do was to stand in front of the altar and receive the blessing. Frankly, I'd had serious doubts about formal religion, but I hadn't run across a guru who had accomplished much for the living standards. I don't go for crouching in a cave. I *was* realistic. I was finishing college, had already accepted a teaching job—roving substitute, three days a week. A lot of my classmates shuddered away from teaching. They couldn't stand the kids, they said. All the lip a teacher takes. Actually, the lippiest students were the biggest shudderers.

When I wasn't teaching, I'd work on my Novel. For the one day a week I saved for my brother Eric, I had already volunteered at Children's Hospital in the city.

I found, in the merry month of May, an apartment within our means. It was great; one of four in a frame building. No complex. Old. Convenient, with a shopping plaza nearby, and not far from the university. The neighborhood was right; a sort of United Nations. All colors and creeds, as the politicians say, and we knew we'd like it. I'd learn how to make shrimp tempura, soul food, and eggdrop soup. At least I hoped I would.

The apartment was partly furnished with a bed and a very overstuffed sofa. Some of the stuffing had burst its bonds. The landlady lived across the hall. She was delighted because I was, and she said an iron-on patch would contain the stuffing. Being allergic to sewing and ironing (I can type), I had never ironed-on a patch, but would give it a try. Anything we needed we could find at the Salvation Army or the Goodwill, or do without.

I guess I really believed that when I got through the preliminaries, I'd be walking up the wide-pictured path into the grove of Grandmother's painting, would lean against the Roman columns, and survey the good scene.

A wedding is a production, starting with the invitations. We forgot to invite Father's cousin, Montgomery Rogers, and his wife, Jane. I don't know how we overlooked the only true troublemakers in the family. A psych. prof would no doubt have an explanation, but nothing that would cool Montgomery or Jane. In a way it was encouraging; marriages have foundered on less than the carnage they were bent on creating.

I was too busy even to think about the path or the grove. There was shopping, which I despise. All those decisions. My wedding gown was beautiful and on sale; Alençon lace over satin, scoop neckline, long sleeves. It had what they called a "cathedral train," and I was afraid I'd stumble over it when I turned. I didn't. Women must be born knowing how to wear a bridal dress. The moment I tried it on, a dream of the far future seemed close enough to touch, and there was hope. Just standing in front of the three-way mirror, I felt so. My veil had been my grandmother's, and it was a mantilla; gossamer—spun sunbeams.

The bouquet was composed of stephanotis and white roses and gypsophila. That's what the florist said. I had never heard of gypsophila; it is pretty and not a disease.

Claire Ordman was my only attendant. She was an English major, naturally, and she offered to design her own wedding costume. I had seen her designs.

"I'll choose the pattern," I told her. "This wedding is straight, all the way."

Claire's dress was golden linen, Empire silhouette. She carried yellow and white daisies, and wore a circlet of daisies in her hair. Looked like Ophelia—fey and sweet. Her shoes were tight, so she eased around in tennis shoes.

At the last minute I noticed she still had on her tennies. I had to think for her, and I will say it took my mind off my own problems. I had never realized Claire was striking; the best man thought she was, too. When he saw her, he looked as if being Mac's army buddy was the best luck he'd ever had, and the trip from Medford worth it. In the golden gown, with her hair a dark cloud, eyes wide and innocent (myopia), Claire was unbelievable.

Especially if you knew her as I did.

When I came down the aisle, it seemed as if Mac and I were alone in the church. His smile trembled as he watched me walk toward him, slowly. We knew love. I prayed, "Please help me to be the kind of person I ought to be."

We had a double-ring ceremony, delayed somewhat when Claire and the best man temporarily forgot they were keepers of the rings.

The reception was in the garden at our house. I saw the loving care of my father and mother. They had planned so the flowers were at their best, and some they had transplanted. Gardens don't just grow; they have to be seeded and bulbed, or whatever, and fertilized, watered, sprayed, pruned, cut, propped up, and thought about. I almost cried because I hadn't realized they were doing all of this for The Day. I knew I had been difficult and a rebel (often unnecessarily), and had frequently nearly driven them over the edge.

The wedding cake was huge. Mother had been baking white fruitcake for two months. Mac and I cut the first piece together. His hand over mine on the knife handle was comforting. A moment before he had seemed a stranger.

Your own wedding is thrilling, and frightening with the knowledge there is no road back to the way it used to be.

When I went upstairs to change, my heart thumped. I was going away forever from the bedroom with the flowered-print curtains and bedspread, and the four-poster, and the dressing table with Eric's picture and my class pictures on it. When I was a little girl I had loved the flowered prints; later on I didn't, but conceded them to Mother because they were camp. Now I was aware there was a kind of security in flowered print that has always been there.

I didn't even know how to iron-on a patch.

Terror made me fumble. Claire had to help me change to my traveling suit; she even buttoned my jacket. I gave the bouquet to her; didn't feel like throwing it.

We were leaving. Mac and I kissed Mother, and he shook hands with Father, and we did the same with his parents. We had borrowed Mac's father's conservative-type transport because we needed room for luggage and odds and ends for the apartment, such as my hope chest; it was small. I hadn't much hope when I started it in the eighth grade. Because it was the parents' car, no funny stuff was done to it, such as rocks in the hubcaps. I thought of Mr. and Mrs. Macfarlane in the M.G.; they gave up dignity for us. And they had a lot of dignity.

It seemed to me I'd always taken from everyone. Never given.

We spent our honeymoon at Mac's aunt's cabin on the lake.

"See?" I said when we got there in the afternoon, late. "She cleaned up."

"She tried." He pulled open a drawer, eyed the forks unhappily. "Egg."

I told him I would wash the silverware. He must have had a very bad experience.

Mother had packed cold cuts and other goodies in a

small foam refrigerator, so I didn't have to fix anything (choc. pudding).

After dinner we sat outside on the falling-down steps in the twilight. As it grew dark, the moon's silver path shimmered across the lake.

I was so happy I felt I might die. And then I thought, Surely most marriages begin like this? What happens? Why do people start un-caring? When?

I whispered, "Mac . . . do you ever think . . . *whither?*"

He kissed me, gently. "No, Katie. I'm sorry. I love you, love you."

But what he said . . . that was whither.

Surely?

2

There are some fine cookbooks, and Mother thoughtfully gave me several. First thing I discovered was you had
to plan ahead. It is terrible thinking about dinner right
after breakfast, but if you don't, at the last minute you find
you should have started an hour earlier. Mac liked to eat
soon after he came home; also, three nights a week he went
back to work at the store, so the meal had to be served on
time. We had forty-five minutes.

In the olden days, so I've heard, working in the retail
business was a life sentence; you saw the sun when you
went to work, and at noon when you brown-bagged it,
weather permitting, behind the store. By midnight you were
lucky if you had the merchandise straightened up for the
early-bird opening; I may be exaggerating slightly, but not
much. Anyway, now the hours are good. There's time off
and the challenge remains. It's hard to believe, but Mac
sometimes wants to stay later than they'll let him.

I had never imagined a business in a plaza would control
my life. It did. Most customers shopped in the evening,
either bringing the children or leaving them home with one
baby-sitting parent. There don't seem to be any maiden

aunts devoting their lives to a young couple's babes, and grandparents are more apt to be swingers than sitters. None of my profs ever mentioned late shopping as a sociological change, but it affected our lives.

Although our dinners were hurried, we visited anyway. I learned a retailer can take a dim view of children.

I like children because they are little people and only notice important things, their eyes being unglazed by the cataracts of propriety. That's why I had always wanted to be a teacher. Children take a lot for granted, such as eating, sleeping, creature comforts, and other people. They are self-centered and sometimes savage; yet rich or poor, black or white are matters of no consequence to them whatsoever. They are themselves. They have freedom of thought, and can believe that hot water is hot because it is so cold (the way I used to), and they think other things that make sense only to them.

Mother tells about the time she and Daddy went shopping with Eric when he was four. It was Christmas week, and Eric had seen several Santas in red velvet and silky whiskers. He was not impressed until he spotted an old man with a long white beard going through the garbage in an alley. Eric tore down the alley shouting, "Santa! Oh, SANTA CLAUS!" It took both my parents to pry him away from the poor old fellow's leg. The man seemed to have the impression that Eric was a boa constrictor and nearly had a fit. Mother said Eric's Santa was suffering a hangover, was bleary-eyed, and smelled to high heaven. No matter. My brother believed.

Mac likes children in a department store if they are closely watched. Children chew on caramels, and may slip a soft one into the pocket of a display dress or down the trouser leg of a new suit. Dripping ice-cream cones ruin the sale of any merchandise they come in contact with, while sticky fingers turn shirt displays gray. Children touch and frequently wind up toys until the spring breaks. Toddlers can choke on anything from earrings snatched from the jewelry counter to merchandise no one but a child could possibly swallow. Mac despises the mothers of unguarded children, and they are legion. He says they don't like their offspring. He is somewhat prejudiced, too, because some small children are in training for shoplifting.

There are mothers who tell their children to "play on the escalator while Mummy shops." You wouldn't believe it. They ought to be held for manslaughter. Escalators are safe, but not foolproof. The sight of a barefooted child on one shatters Mac's nerves; he can't stand the thought of a toeless kid.

One has to be careful. If a little one is snatched away from something lethal, the result may be gallons of tears on the child's part, and it can also arouse the tiger in the mother, something to be avoided at all costs. The tiger is very near the surface in a mother, even an indifferent one.

Little Adolph's mother was a case in point. She was so round you couldn't tell whether she was walking or rolling, and six-year-old Adolph was almost as tall as she. While he was only practicing to be a monster, Mac says, she had already developed into one. Fierce. Whenever Little Adolph and his mother advanced upon Mac's department, he broke out in a sweat.

Little Adolph's specialty was to push boxes of merchandise off the counters as he walked beside his mother. He was particularly fond of sock boxes, since there were so many and they made a lovely mess. Mac tried everything from the icy glare to the firm hand on the shoulder, at which point Adolph would shout, "Mama!"

And she would say, "*Here* I am, Little Adolph."

They were never more than a foot apart. You had to grant her that.

But one day Adolph was operating at full capacity, pushing sock boxes, and was temporarily disengaged from Mama. Mac got on the opposite side of the table and when Adolph pushed, Mac pushed *back*, giving Adolph a brisk blow on the jaw. Adolph screamed, and to quiet him Mama gave him a clout on the ear. Fortunately, he was yelling so hard Mama couldn't figure out what happened. In a semi-crouch Mac got away from the scene of the crime, and presently advanced to wait on them from the other direction. While Adolph was not able to explain, he knew what he knew; he was suspicious of smiling Mac, and wary. Mac says it is too soon to say Adolph has reformed, but at least he seems to believe sock boxes have a life of their own.

It takes a great deal of thought to improve a situation such as Adolph's. Mac is modest about it; he says better men than he had failed. He was lucky.

At breakfast Mac and I moved, chewed, and spoke quietly, since he greeted the dawn with no enthusiasm. But our dinner conversations were unbelievable. I had never known there were so many problems in the retail business.

For example, stealing. Some people will steal anything. The store calls stolen merchandise "shrinkage." *I* think of it as rent and food, and take it personally. In the J. C. Penney Company we are *part* of the company, not just employees. Who steals from our store, steals from us. Penneys has a share-in-the-profit plan (Mr. J. C. Penney had started it in the early days); if a great deal is stolen, there *is* no profit. The markup is small, and the saving is passed to the customer. Theft causes costs to rise. Everyone loses.

I have taken to *hating* the jerks who steal for kicks. I even hate little kids who do it. And I include in this the parents, who must know; if they don't recognize new merchandise that they have not given the children money for, they shouldn't raise a family in the first place. Of course, some of the parents steal, too. Mac says most people are honest. I am not sure. A nice, tough judge is just the one to point out to people who make a career of this sort of thing that jail is their future.

There was a time I believed some people were kleptomaniacs. There may be a few. "Maybe they can't help themselves," I told Mac.

"The judge can decide about that," said Mac, showing a lot of teeth. "I've never *met* a kleptomaniac; all I've seen are damned thieves." Mac has hardened because he is worn out with liars and thieves. He does not care for them, and doesn't care what the judge does with them, either.

"My psych. prof said stores made merchandise so attractive—you know, fancy displays and all that jazz—that some people feel they have a *right* to take whatever they want. They can't resist it."

Mac's voice was mean-soft when he answered. "So *you're* a prize package, Katie. So some guy wants you. He takes you?"

"Surely you don't equate merchandise with a person!"

"I equate stealing anything that doesn't belong to you with criminal intent. From goods to people is a half step, and one that is easy to take."

I disagreed with him then, but now I don't know, because it's complicated. If a burglar tried to take our TV set, the only thing of value we have, and are still paying for (except the pans), he'd have to fight me. Probably I'd lose;

maybe I'd be killed. But I'm sure I'd fight. So I—a human being—am involved with violence. I don't like it.

At the very least, thieves deserve a good fright.

The way the store provided a fright (and sometimes something more serious) was by means of detectives. These people are often merchandise retirees or off-duty guards or moonlighting policemen, and they are accustomed to *noticing*. Experience does it. Mac can tell when a shopper has on tuck-stitch shoplifter's bloomers, and he takes a dim view of big boxes, overlarge raincoats and shopping bags that come in empty and go out full. There are other gambits.

Mac says he can smell a thief.

There was a lady detective named Mrs. Sutler who had a marvelous record. I had never met anyone in my life who made so little impression. She was almost invisible, for some reason; no one ever saw her, including me. She was not tall and not fat or thin, and her eyes were merely eyes. Her whole system was like that, which was probably the reason she nabbed shoplifters constantly. She hated them; she had had a very hard life and had not stooped to stealing, and didn't know why anyone else would. However, she didn't look as if she hated anyone, because she had no expression. You couldn't possibly have guessed she knew karate blows that reduced those she pursued to wrecks, which may sound awful, but was something she enjoyed.

I had a very embarrassing experience with Mrs. Sutler. Mac had introduced her to me on the lower level where he worked (basement). I went up to first floor and spoke to a woman I vaguely recognized. Did the same on second floor, third, and fourth, and on the fifth floor this mousy individual hissed, "*Will* you stop attracting attention?"

Oh, steady on.

She was following a case, and I almost blew the whole

thing. I was so unnerved I went straight home. I had not realized Mrs. Sutler kept a different sweater and/or hat and/or coat and shoes and purse on every floor. I merely thought I had seen her someplace before, and I had.

If she walked into the room right this minute, I wouldn't know her. And if she went on into the next room and came back, I'd have forgotten she ever went *in*. It was a good thing she was on our side.

People like Mrs. Sutler keep down the thief population, and even if I never do know who she is, I am grateful.

We had good dinner conversations, but menus for our on-the-dot meals drove me up the wall. Steaks and chops (quick cookers I'd need when I started my job) were expensive; TV dinners were what Mac had as a kid when he was being punished. That left macaroni, tough roasts (which I found out how to tenderize), spaghetti, and variations made from ground meat. I once made hash from a tough roast, and the hash was tough, too, believe it or not. We chewed and chewed, and I told Mac about the time I was served bits of octopus at a cocktail party, and likewise chewed. I must have gotten the suction cups or whatever. At the least, they were vulcanized. Mac turned sort of chartreuse, and I stopped talking about octopus. We had a lot of hash left over that night.

There was a certain sameness about the food we could afford, even in rotation. I managed a budget-type steak from time to time. I still had a problem. Mac prefers his well cooked, and I like mine rare. I overdid it both ways. Mac didn't mention it then, but later he said that all during July whatever meat I cooked tasted like and looked like *hoof*. He once examined my steak, turned pale, and muttered we ought to tether it in the back yard.

Although I had all day to think about dinner (roving

sub-teaching began in September), I never seemed able to finish vegetables, meat, and salad at the same time, and when I did they were then ready at exactly the same moment and it was a race to get them on the table. Rushing that way, I once poured vegetable water on the lettuce and threw the peas in the sink. When I had been living with my parents or going to restaurants or eating at the dorm, I had not realized how complicated it was to prepare a meal. It may be significant that Mother had preferred to do the cooking, while I changed the beds and cleaned.

Mac said not to worry; consider the first two months boot camp. I brooded, because I recalled some of his other comments on boot camp. He then pointed out there were certain differences and chased me around the apartment. Caught me easily.

The landlady, Mrs. Swensen, knocked at the door one evening when Mac was working, and I confided that I was a failure in the food department. The night before, I'd put garlic in the meatloaf thinking it was a variety of onion, and Mac had a miserable encounter with a well-coiffured, up-tight matron who snarled that salesmen who ate garlic ought to be arrested. Until that moment, Mac hadn't known what was the matter with him. The public will say anything.

One mistake we were not likely to make was taking a serious interest in the booze scene. In the retail business, employees who join the martini-at-lunch circuit are let go the moment they become members of the club, or the day before. Customers react with fantastic speed to bourbon whiffs, and they can sniff out the vermouth in a vodka martini as soon as the culprit has poured it down the hatch. Even with no odor to go by, a potential buyer is put off by a gait with a loop in it. Customers don't communicate their disgust to the man or woman on the floor, either; they go right to the boss. That's *it*. Retailers who think they can relax before dinner with a Scotch and soda and then go to work at the plaza, or have a friendly bottle of wine at the evening meal and sell socks later, will find themselves hoping for unemployment benefits. There are other fields where this antipolicy applies: medicine, dentistry, you name it. From jet pilots to bus drivers, drinking on the job is a disaster area. Could be my family was right to be suspicious of alcoholic beverages. They didn't forbid them on special occasions, but they were careful. My mother once got excited about a bottle of root beer I was drinking, and Father had to read the label to her in a loud voice four times before she was convinced it would not give me the blind staggers. Naturally, I had a hangup about alcohol. It took the form of extreme caution.

Garlic was undesirable, but not a fatal offense. I felt unbelievably moronic about serving several buttons to trusting Mac. Mrs. Swensen said I was not stupid, but merely lacked experience. I hoped she was right. Since her husband had been in the navy, she explained I was on my shakedown cruise. It sounded better than boot camp. It had always seemed to me that cooking was simple; if you could read, you could cook. Not so. I began to take an increasing interest in women who never learned to cook—there are articles about them in the magazines: actresses, wives of important men, and slobs. The only category I had a chance of making was slob, and I decided, despite definite tendencies, I would not be one. There was another point: How did those women get away with *not* cooking? I mean, they liked to *eat* didn't they? Who *did* it? Husbands? The delicatessen? Restaurants? The Salvation Army?

Mrs. Swensen made up a chart for me so I'd know what to do first. Doing first things first is a good idea in home-making—when you can make the decision as to what is first. I washed the baseboards every day. I developed a thing about them, and when I saw a filthy baseboard some-where else it gave me a lift. You'd be surprised how many people don't think of baseboards at all; and ours were in plain sight because we had so little furniture. However, I could not make up my mind whether to start by dusting the furniture (the dirt would then fall on the baseboard, and you could clean that), or cleaning the floors. I saw I was becoming compulsive-obsessive, so after a while I quit thinking. Probably that's the way it is with any job; get on with it. No one else is going to do it for you, that you can be sure of. One of the worst discoveries about marriage is that it's up to you.

So I scrubbed and polished and washed and otherwise knocked myself out.

Often when I was slaving, I would grunt, "Will this marriage *last?*" I could see weary years ahead. Sometimes I'd sit back from scrubbing and wipe my brow (leaving a dark streak that was fairly satisfactory, but could have been better; I went over the entire place every day), and I would fan a flame of hatred for people who walked on clean floors. Sometimes I'd daydream, and that was best. It made the time speed by, as long as I didn't forget com-pletely what I was doing. I'd conjure up a small income from someone or other. For example, my father's uncle had gone to the Yukon to make his fortune, and had disap-peared. My father said his uncle disappeared because his wife had been a natural shrew from birth, and after mar-riage she developed into a dedicated shrew. Anyway, my uncle was probably an old, lonely millionaire by now . . . very old. I figured about one hundred and six. He would be charmed if he could see me; he certainly would. So there I'd be with an income.

Or I'd imagine myself strolling around an English manor, basket on arm (one of those curved ones with a graceful handle), shears in hand, cutting long-stemmed, thornless tea roses, which the gardener had grown. I do not have a green thumb and am sure I will never develop one. My favorite dream was the one where I saw myself sitting cozily with the cook, outlining meals for the next fortnight. Usually as I got going on this one, a cramp would attack me, or I'd back into the scrub bucket, slopping. I'd start grunting again. It was some comfort to reflect that it was difficult for anyone to obtain domestic help. (In dreams the cooks, etc., were old retainers; in my family we were more apt to *be* the old retainer than have one. The wonder of a dream is you can do anything.) Since help was hard to find, women across the country were either doing as I was, or they lived in a state of mess and microbes.

You know those ladies' magazines with full pages of a *femme* in tailored wash and wear smilingly painting a chair, or happily holding out a can of cleaner—gleaming woodwork in the background? Or laughingly salting the stew? Some Madison Avenue male makes up those ads; he's not married. When I am occupied with these duties, I look like the Before in a Before-and-After advertisement. Moreover, I found that clever decorating ideas demand financial leeway; we did not have it. We were poor but clean. I could only be grateful that I never identified with the little match girl. That is, I cried buckets over the story, but I certainly would have tried to get out of the blizzard. Somehow.

Despite lack of money, I invested in some paint. It was amazing. I painted one closet and found that when I did the ceiling, the paint ran down to my elbow. When I kept on painting, it dribbled to the armpit. Yellow armpits. No wonder Michelangelo lay flat on his back to do a ceiling. When I had the yellow armpits I hoped there wouldn't be a fire; I might develop into an interesting medical case. My mother always worried about her underwear in case of fire, but I worried about yellow armpits; they would confuse the emergency staff of the hospital. I was pleased with the closet, and I got another small can of paint and did the kitchen shelves. After I finished the top one, painting underneath for an extra fine job, I started on the next shelf. Well, I was working back and forth, rubbing my head against the (forgotten) wet paint on the underside, when my brain clicked. I came out of there very fast. Sure enough. Pink-top. I was going to pour turpentine on my head, but Mrs. Swensen said my hair would fall out. She cotton-wiped each hair—oh, maybe five at a time. I have Mrs. Swensen to thank for not achieving premature baldness.

It came to me that I had always taken a great deal for granted. Like buttons. Mac asked me to sew a button on his shirt. I did not have one. We had not accumulated strays. For several days, I removed a button from one shirt to another, but it got on Mac's nerves. Finally I went to the Variety Store and tried to buy two buttons. They didn't sell only two. Carried away by my resolution never again to be buttonless, I bought twenty. It would have been a good start on a button box, if we'd had one. Mac told me they sold buttons at the store; in fact, in his department. I could have bought them there for less. Whenever I discover I might have bought something for less, I am plunged into an intense gloom.

There is also the problem of rags. A good rag is more precious than rubies. Well, anyway, a nice rag is desirable, and you can't make much of a rag out of a washcloth, although I did—from a puce-colored one Claire had given us. At Mrs. Swensen's suggestion, I invested in some sponges. Also got some throwaway paper towels that you use as rags, but could not bring myself to throw away the throwaways. All these problems were demoralizing. I was not raised in a vacuum, but there was much I did not know. Which reminds me: we did not have a vacuum cleaner. We had a carpet sweeper.

Then there are shirts. Though they were drip-dry, I always pressed Mac's shirts to get out small wrinkles; when Mac left in the mornings—fresh shave, shower, clean shirt (pressed), soft socks—I was proud. He looked so great. I developed an inferiority complex in shorts and blouse. Mother had told me how it was in the old days: the first shirt she ironed was corrugated when she finished because there were no steam irons and after an hour of struggle, the material was wrinkled again. I was grateful for drip-dry shirts, and I was especially grateful I didn't have to make shirts, the way my grandmother had. I'd have probably ended up with a smock. Sewing was a required subject in the seventh grade; I was the only one who had to redo a French seam (practicing on a dish towel) five times. In between tries, I had to wash the towel because of my honest, seventh-grade, grubby sweat. I took to entertaining the girls at my table out of boredom, and the home-ec teacher said if I didn't keep quiet she would put me in the closet. I knew it would be the sort of punishment my parents would applaud (they were always on the teacher's side), so I shut up and redid the seam.

Naturally, I tried to conceal my inadequacies from the groom, but I told Mrs. Swensen *all*. She was so understanding she didn't even laugh when she came in and found me cooking spaghetti in a long pan, stirring frequently; I wanted long spaghetti, you see, and had never heard you could sort of melt the ends in a round pan until the whole batch slid into the water in a circle. How would I know that? How *would* I? My mother did not like spaghetti.

Mrs. Swensen was one of the darlingest people ever born. She had rosy cheeks and white hair and heaven-sent blue eyes, and she had a way of chuckling that made you feel great because she was laughing at life, not you. I don't know how other brides get along without a Mrs. Swensen. I'll try to be like her, someday; might do more lasting good than social work . . . generation to generation, passing down recipes, rags, and common sense. It would be desirable, also, to be small and trim the way she was, although fat and chuckling wouldn't be bad. It's the chuckle that counts.

A bride and groom are like lost children; they need some attention, but from someone outside the family, since families think they own their children forever. ("Don't you think you'd better get a sweater?" "What gave you the rash?" "Surely you aren't making a public appearance in *that?*")

In addition to Mrs. Swensen, we had a lot going for us in the other tenants. There were four apartments in the building. The Swensens and Macfarlanes (us) occupied the first-floor apartments, and Mary and Bill Shaw, and Sue and Romeo Campagna lived on the second floor. Romeo had a love-hate relationship with his first name. He liked the romantic connotation ("A great lover," he said), but hated to hear, "O Romeo, Romeo! wherefore art thou Romeo?" So we called him "Whuffor." He preferred it.

There was a little fenced-in yard in back of the apartment. On hot summer nights we sat on the grass and talked and argued and laughed. The Swensens never joined us, but they could hear everything, the windows wide open. Sometimes I heard Mrs. Swensen chuckle, and Mr. Swensen moan, "Yah, Sharlie." We had picnics out there, too, but could not grill. The neighbors objected to our pollution. So we grilled inside and ate on the lawn on the nights Mac didn't go to work. Later we had iced tea or lemonade, and when we felt rich (rarely) a highball. Trouble was, they made us hotter. I'd never turn alcoholic in the tropics, but I'd definitely fall apart; swing in a hammock all day, all night.

The neighbors on one side were antipollution (they thought *we* polluted), and on the other side there lived a three-year-old we called "The Screamer." Whenever things went against him, he screamed. Things went against him all the time, particularly bedtime. Whuffor thought he'd be a grand-opera star someday, if he lived that long. Whuffor was an enormous, kind man; he had played football at the university and was six feet tall, but looked shorter because he was also wide. All muscle, he said. One night he took out his teeth (the four front teeth are almost always sacrificed to varsity football), and I considered disappearing for three or four days. He had large brown spaniel eyes, curly black hair. Sue was, predictably, blonde and blue-eyed, had dimples and, as Mac noticed, "a terrific bod." She was very, very funny without meaning to be, and was gentle.

Mary Shaw was tall; violet eyes, black hair, and that gorgeous Irish complexion, snow white. She never tanned, but burned and peeled. She was classically beautiful and had no idea of it. She was always thinking of going on a diet, but never did. Actually, Mary was voluptuous. She didn't realize that, either. Bill Shaw had finished medical school and was in third-year residency, psychiatry. He was generally unimpressed with himself, but was proud of his glossy brown, handle-bar moustache. He said the only thing he couldn't stand about Mary was when he would come home from a hard day with the psychiatric patients (and he was determined to save every single one, even if they were happy Napoleons), Mary would start a typical Irish argument by saying, "The trouble with *you* is . . ."

The only statement a psychiatrist can't bear to hear is, "The trouble with *you* is . . ." Actually, Bill was bright and nice and sensible—a very unusual about-to-be psychiatrist. When they got around to having children, we were sure they would not be mixed up. I mean the children. What Mary couldn't stand about Bill was he had a tendency to use her for various tests and occasionally, she discovered, discussed her as a hypothetical case with the interns. It made her very cross.

We all liked each other, and there was no flirty-girty stuff. That was a middle-aged syndrome, Bill Shaw said, and one we ought always to avoid.

Mrs. Swensen chose the tenants. She liked young people, and she had a knack for choosing compatibles. Better than a computer, I told her. Actually, we didn't see each other as much as we would have liked. Mary worked. Sue did, too, in a travel agency. She once sent a customer to Bristol, Indiana, when he wanted to go to Bristol, Pennsylvania, but by the time he returned she dimpled at him, and he got over his rage. Whuffor was in his father's food-broker-age business, and after we really got acquainted he brought us vegetables that had started to spoil outside but were edible inside.

For a while, there, I was the only one at home with the

46

Swensens. Neither the teaching nor the hospital-volunteer work in memory of Eric started until September. It was just as well; I needed to make adjustments. I was the only English major in the group.

Sue told us the people who'd lived in our apartment before we came had been one of Mrs. Swensen's rare mistakes. They were hung up on beer, complete with burps, bellies, and bombast. Whuffor came from a large family, and he hired his twelve-year-old twin cousins to clump around the living room all night for several weeks, in wooden sandals. Took up the rug first. The cousins divided the clumping into shifts, and the Beer Baron and Baroness gave notice. Everyone said they were sorry to see them go, so their egos would not be depleted, and at the last minute they almost decided to stay, but Whuffor brought in two young nieces and paid them to giggle all night. That did it.

Whuffor helped the Beer Baron pack, borrowed his uncle's truck, and got them settled across town. It was a good solution for everyone.

The apartments were not soundproof, not at that price; but we tried to keep the decibels down. We took to brushing our teeth *lightly;* for some reason, you could hear tooth-brushing better than anything else. Whuffor made less noise than the rest of us; fewer teeth. However, he was disappointed because with the front bridge he couldn't bite the top off a pineapple; in fact, I didn't believe it. I called him Romeo for the rest of the evening when he became bitter about pineapple one summer night. When we were not on the best of terms, we all called him Romeo.

Another interesting item was that our keys unlocked each other's doors. We hadn't tried the Swensens, but were reasonably sure it was four out of four. This was to come in handy.

I was anxious for school to start; felt like a parasite. Yet it was a learning period for me and, among other things, I learned to love Mrs. Swensen dearly. About Mr. Swensen I was neutral, which in itself was an accomplishment.

I experimented with the iron-on patches on the sofa. They looked like iron-on patches, or even more so. We bought some madly colored throws, and although guests who sat on the middle cushion had a tendency to look startled, thinking they had developed instant tumor, the job was satisfactory. Almost everything worked out.

We were saving money for a house. We kept it in the flour bin, in a plastic bag; more subtle than the teapot or the cookie jar. "Good place for dough," said Mac. "Ha."

After the bread-baking attempt, I didn't have much use for flour anyway, and the bin was a good place for money because it was a lot of trouble to get it out. You thought twice before you dug down and ended up looking like ye old jolly miller. The bread I baked when we had twenty cents left didn't rise. Mrs. Swensen said it squatted to rise and baked in the squat. Mac suggested we use the loaf for the cornerstone in our future house. He was fairly insensitive about that sort of thing.

We would not borrow money; we were afraid of overextending ourselves. We had read a book on the subject of debt. The cases were from real life, and they were horrendous. One man had a nervous breakdown because his wages were garnisheed. The way interest could pile up was unbelievable. A wife killed herself over interest. What we learned from the book was to do without. Also, the J. C. Penney Company encouraged moderation in everything.

I don't know why it is that I learn mainly through my mistakes; reading about them is real enough, but I always think I'll be different.

I was at low ebb one day because there had been a sock in the white-clothes washing. We'd bought our own equipment instead of patronizing a Laundromat, although people had a good time at pay wash-and-dries and picked up useful information. Friends called the Laundromat "The Club." Since the sock that inadvertently got in with the white clothes was red, everything came out in various shades of pink. I was sure Mac would not go for streaked pink shorts, although who would know? (What if there was a *fire?*)

I went next door to consult Mrs. Swensen. She wasn't home, but her husband was. Mr. Swensen was a good man, even though grumpy. He tried not to be cross. He went to church—fundamentalist—and he prayed over his disposition. Nothing worked. Without doubt he had married Mrs. Swensen because she was sweet; he certainly wouldn't put up with anyone like himself.

I told Mr. Swensen about the sock and he said, "Yah, Sharlie. Yoost like a woman." He shut the door.

Mr. Swensen always said "Yah, Sharlie" when under stress. It was his way of swearing, and effective because that's how he meant it.

When he shut the door firmly (slammed it), I went desolately back to our apartment. The sock was my fault, but those machines ought to be smart enough to reason. The washer sort of buzzed when the load was too big, and the dryer honked when finished. Both the washer and dryer sounded so anguished when they let out with these calls that I ran like a madwoman when doing the laundry, before they could suffer more.

I kicked the washing machine when I got back because it was color blind. I knew it was a cruel thing to do. Then I kicked the tumorous davenport because I felt like it.

When I heard chimes I thought it was the washer crying.

49

Maybe the davenport. I was nervous until it came to me that someone was at the door. I answered, and a man was holding out a teakettle. Before I had a chance to say a word, he explained I had been chosen to receive a gift.

It was the first good thing that had happened all day. The gift was steel and copper. Beautiful. And free. I was speechless.

"I wonder if I could trouble you for a glass of water?" he asked, after I had taken the kettle in my nerveless fingers.

"Surely," I told him, and brought one. It was a hot day, and he looked too exhausted to be a strangler.

We got to talking, and it turned out he was in the pots-and-pans business. I didn't have any to speak of, and no sturdy ones at all. He thought that was why I was having trouble cooking. He said he had a recipe book that simplified everything. As a matter of fact, he had happened to put the entire line of pans in his car that morning, so he'd just run out and get a few to show to me, as well as the recipe book.

He introduced himself; his name was Henry Clift. He made several trips to the car. There were pots of every description on the chairs, on the counter—all steel and copper. We visited a long time.

Five dollars down, and five dollars a week. It was lucky they were having a special. At the same time, it was a miracle I had five dollars for a down payment; I'd been saving it for Mac's birthday. When I started teaching I'd have money, and it would all be paid for in only fifty weeks.

Mr. Clift decided he'd better leave the whole order right then. He trusted me. His eyes sparkled when he said there was something he had been saving for a surprise. I would receive, as a bonus for buying, and absolutely free, a portable sewing machine. Well! I forgot about my troubles in the seventh grade, and when I did remember, I realized I had never concentrated before. Besides a complete instruction and pattern book came with the machine.

After Mr. Clift left, both of us waving good-by like old friends, I went on with the housework as if I had wings. The sewing machine would be delivered the next Monday, and Mac would be pleased some night when he came home and found me finishing a fine seam. I did realize there were a few items in my new supply of pans that I wouldn't need right away, such as the colander. It would be useful in the future, I was sure. Meanwhile, I had one.

After the baseboards were washed, I arranged the items on the kitchen counter in stacks, a sort of store display I thought would please Mac. Store display?

I was stunned. Maybe I could have gotten all those pans at our store, with a discount. This realization was followed by another blow: probably my father would have sold us the stuff at cost. I recalled, however, that Mr. Clift had said this particular marvelous set could only be purchased through specialized salesmen. I felt better but did not regain my former high.

The outside door slammed. I knew it was Mrs. Swensen, and I called to her. She came in and stood in the dinette, her eyes wide.

"Don't you like them?"

"Oh, they're lovely," she said. "So many . . . I never had that many in all my life."

I stared at her and panic began to spread throughout my nerve endings, or wherever it is panic spreads.

She put her arm around me and said again, "Lovely. Just lovely."

"I hope Mac goes for steel and copper."

"If he doesn't, you can return them."

That made me more nervous. "I don't think so. There was a contract. I signed."

"How old are you, Katie?"

"Old enough to know better," I said, suddenly bitter. "Twenty-one."

"It's legal, then." She brightened. "Never you mind. It's a good investment."

"Let's show them to Mr. Swensen."

"I don't believe . . ."

But I couldn't wait; I needed reserves. I ran across the hall and brought him back with me. I kept babbling on and on about my bargain, but he seemed too surprised to react.

Mrs. Swensen said, "Men don't appreciate cookingware."

Mr. Swensen acted as if the pots and pans were equipment for the moon, shook his head, hitched his trousers, snapped his suspenders, and started to back out the door.

"What do you *think?*" I asked desperately.

He gave a bark, which in Mr. Swensen passed for laughter. He said, "Gonna be up to your—yah, Sharlie!—in pots and pans."

That did it.

I started shaking, hard.

Mrs. Swensen bustled around and found the tea bags; I managed to put on the pan I'd used for heating water. I couldn't bear to sully the new one.

The tea was calming, but unease had grown into terror. "Do you think . . . grounds for divorce?"

"Now, now . . ." Mrs. Swensen patted my shoulder. "Why don't you put all the things in the cupboards and bring out one piece at a time, when you feel it would be tactful?"

"May not be space enough." That was another problem, and I shook harder.

We found, by careful stacking, there was. That is, nothing showed when Mac came home that night. I was lying down resting my eyes and calming my conscience.

Mac isn't the type who says, "What's the matter?" He just offers pleasant, silent sympathy and figures if there is something wrong, he'll be told about it. I dragged through dinner, toyed with my food. I'd never appreciated the phrase "toyed with my food." That's what you do—play with it, push it from place to place on the plate.

When I was doing the dishes, I had an idea. I took in one of the new pans as Mac was reading and relaxing on the lumpy sofa. He glanced at it and nodded. "We have them at the store."

I collapsed in a heap. I would have to tell. Maybe there was a better way, but I didn't know what it was.

"A man came to the door today and, Mac . . . oh, Mac . . ." I started to cry; I couldn't go on.

He jumped up and came over to me. "Katie, what happened?"

I was crying, and I had a headache, and, oh, I don't know, I couldn't say anything.

He started pacing around, making fists. "Where'd he go?"

I said, "Mrs. Swensen."

Mac went out, then. Pretty soon he came back with Mrs. Swensen. I heard her open a cupboard door. I blew my nose and waited.

Mrs. Swensen and Mac had a conversation, in low tones. She left and he came into the living room, sat down beside me.

"Don't ever start like that when you have something to tell me," he said in a tight voice.

"I'm sorry," I whispered.

"I thought you'd been hurt, Katie. Now I find it's pots and pans."

"I signed a contract."

"I know."

"What came over me?"

"Those salesmen are trained," he said slowly. "More experienced buyers than you are can't resist what they think is a bargain. Look at it this way, Katie: maybe the pans will keep you from buying a gold brick someday, or a nonproducing oil well. It isn't a bad product, either, just overpriced. Meanwhile, we have housewares, God knows, and you will have to figure the budget."

Fifty weeks stretched ahead of me. My life wasn't exactly blighted, but it is tiring to have pots and pans on your mind. Worse than baseboards.

There were two good results from Mr. Clift's visit. One: Mac had let me know that not even money was as important as I was; and two: I, who had been disdainful of money, found out it was important when translated into fringe living and five dollars a week. For once I appreciated the business point of view. Money may be only a word, but whether you think of it as colored beads for trade, or pots—yah, Sharlie!—you can't ignore it.

There are many small ways to economize, and I learned about them. Canceled our subscription to the morning newspaper, ironed the Swensens' when they were finished so the pages were all crisp and fresh-looking for Mac. After he read it, before dinner, I would return the paper to Mrs. Swensen for garbage. I missed the listing of evening activities, but I could always listen to the radio. Mrs. Swensen had the idea about the paper; Mr. Swensen didn't know about it. However, I was experiencing difficulty with garbage disposal. I'd taken paper for granted, just like a lot of other things. I needed it to wrap garbage in. There was, of course, the shopping news (a throwaway) and supermarket specials, free. Whenever I went for a walk and saw a newspaper blowing around, I'd pursue it. I wasn't crazy about the paper chase, but garbage is ever present. There is lots of it, even for two people. I'd never thought about garbage, any more than I'd appreciated a button. (Oh, sure, I understood the importance of industrial waste disposal, but I didn't equate that with *mine*.)

There is that old poem about the kingdom lost for want of a horseshoe nail. Small things can be important. The shoe fell off, the horse fell down, and the rider broke his neck, or something. Anyway, he couldn't deliver a vital message, all for want of a horseshoe nail. A button could be a horseshoe nail, symbolically speaking. A handkerchief, too; I remember Winston Beall in the sixth grade when he recited a beautiful poem and had a cold and no handkerchief. *That* was a lost cause.

I guess I have mentioned we were paying for the TV set in installments. Living color. For entertainment we had TV, Mac's old radio, our friends, and everything that was free: museums, parks, the public library, parades, and friends. We had floor cushions scattered around for people who came to see us, plus the davenport. We were comfortable. And I don't mean to belabor the poverty bit, because we weren't poor; we just didn't have much money. When I started my job, there would be more.

We had everything we needed, and almost all we wanted. We were not in Chaucer's situation when he complained to his empty purse: "Beth hevy agen, or elles moote I dye."

It is too bad the outside world has to interfere, but the life of Herman the Hermit would not be for me. Mac was a handy man with a hammer; on his days off, he put up shelves and fixed things. He was mechanically inclined and spent hours tuning up the M.G. There wasn't anything wrong with it, but it was old and tired and a classic. M.G. stands for Morris Garages; I had no idea until Mac told me, and also the car was valuable. Money in the bank.

I don't believe all the best things in life are free, but some are. We had no sex problems, so we didn't need to invest in a how-to book. Mac said people who knew no joy and couldn't figure out how to needed a head shrink, not a book. Maybe. At any rate, we didn't need to check the page or the paragraph. Steady on, and what a gift!

And right here I should say something about that tenderness. We tried to be good to each other. Every morning Mac said, "Have I told you today I love you?" And—I know it sounds silly—but when I heard his footsteps coming along the sidewalk to the apartment or his voice speaking to someone outside, my heart shook with delight.

Oh, Mac . . .

Oh, Katie . . .

Us. Us. Together.

We touched—we kissed hello, kissed good-by. I wished I could live in his pocket just to be close, always. The buttons were love, the cooking was love . . . the baseboards. And when he brought home his paycheck, it was love that he gave me—working hard, long, for us.

We loved.

My father had been concerned because he thought we wouldn't know anyone. We knew more people than we could handle; a handy man always has friends. Our apartment neighbors were terrific, and we figured we'd always know each other. Then there was Randolph.

Mac met Randolph first when he was working on the M.G., which he dearly loved and was lucky to have because it was a T.C. That's a special type M.G. Randolph was interested initially in Mac's legs sticking out from under the car. Then they found they had something more in common: baseball. Randolph loved baseball; no one wanted him to play, but he did, anyway. There was a vacant lot down the street; children gathered there every night during good weather. Randolph was an outfielder. The trouble was he ran away with the ball, which drove everyone crazy because there was only one ball. Randolph was a standard French poodle, the size of a small horse. We knew his name because it was on a collar tag. He was walnut-colored, including his eyes. He did not have a poodle cut; he looked like an enormous mop. When Randolph fielded, and finally disengaged the wet ball after pleading and pursuit, the pitcher had a problem: he was accused of throwing spitballs. One night, after much outcry, Randolph took fright and, pursued by the losing team, located our apartment. I invited him in. He sighed and flopped, and we were his refuge ever after.

The first time Mr. Swensen saw Randolph, he thought he was seeing a bear. The circumstances were unusual. Mr. Swensen thought the bear was hugging me in a death embrace when, in fact, I was trying to teach Randolph not to jump up on people, because he knocked them down and might accidentally fracture someone's skull. When Randolph jumped that day, I had grabbed his forepaws, and we were doing a sort of slow waltz, which I believe Randolph enjoyed. Actually, I was attempting to step on his back paws, but Randolph would have none of that—so we advanced and backed up, and progressed around the back yard in rather dignified fashion, really.

Mr. Swensen let out with a screech that frightened both Randolph and me, and left Mr. Swensen totally depleted.

Often things are not what they seem to be.

Mr. Swensen collapsed slowly on the back step and stared into space, thinking. After a while he said, "Yours?"

"My friend."

I had released Randolph and, never one to hold a grudge, he went over and licked Mr. Swensen's nose. I have not mentioned Mr. Swensen's nose, but it was sort of a button. As a matter of fact, it looked like Randolph's, except that it became crimson when he was annoyed, which was almost always.

"Mugwumph," said Mr. Swensen. Randolph was licking and trying to sit in his lap.

I went to our apartment.

It was a wonder they had never met before, but Mr. Swensen was not one to neighbor. Randolph had a loving heart, so he put Mr. Swensen on his route. I think he fell in love with Mr. Swensen's nose. Evenings after Randolph had been put out of the ball game, they made quite a sight, sitting on the back step side by side, Mr. Swensen and Randolph. They never spoke; just sat, with Randolph moving ever closer to Mr. Swensen, who really didn't need the additional warmth of Randolph's fur coat. So Mr. Swensen would edge away and inevitably fall off the step into the juniper bush, with Randolph, in apology and pity, licking his face as he tried to arise. Mr. Swensen couldn't even say, "Yah, Sharlie!" because he had to keep his mouth shut. Randolph salivated excessively when emotional. Mr. Swensen would wipe off his face with one of the blue bandanas he always carried, sit on the step again, and the whole process would begin once more, but slowly. We counted three episodes one evening and had to go into our apartments, although it was hot; but no one cared to offend Mr. Swensen. He could not stand to be laughed at. The juniper bush was large and rather flat, and when Mr. Swensen landed in it he resembled a turtle on its back. He couldn't get up, especially with Randolph offering succor.

It was the afternoon when Randolph and I tripped the light fantastic that Mary Shaw had her crisis. I was thinking about dinner and alert to the time when I heard a low call. It seemed to come from one of the second-floor apartments. I went up the stairs, and sure enough—from the Shaws' apartment—"Help!"

I tried the door; it was locked. Ran downstairs and got my key, opened the door.

Following moans, groans, and some bad language, I advanced to the bathroom. "What's the matter?"

"Who's there?"

"Katie."

"Oh."

"Shall I get Mr. Swensen?"

"NO! God, no. Oh, I can't bear it."

"What?"

Sepulchral tones. "I cannot get up."

"You want a doctor?"

"No."

"Mary, what *is* it?" I thought one of the customers had chased Mary around the table again. It was always happening, and she was always astonished, but quick and young and full of energy. Depending upon the number of laps around, she would be either in a good mood or desperate. Now she sounded so desperate that I thought she had probably spent the afternoon jogging around a table. Of course, her psychiatrist husband suggested many possible techniques for avoiding the chase, including wearing Mother Hubbards to work. But on her, a Mother Hubbard would look sexy.

The door opened two inches. "Mr. Swensen enameled the toilet seat today," said Mary. "While I was working."

"Oh, God," I said.

"Thick enamel. Get Mrs. Swensen."

"She isn't here."

"I'll kill myself."

"You can't, at the moment," I said. "Look, I have some turpentine from when I painted my hair. . . ."

"You painted your hair?" Even in Mary's extremity, she was intellectually curious, one of the things I liked about her.

"Naturally, I didn't mean to. I was doing the shelves."

The door swung open. It looked to me as if Mary had settled down for all time.

"I was reading a book," she said, "and stayed longer than I intended, and then . . ."

"Yes. Wait where you are."

"Don't worry." She was sarcastic, but after all I was only trying to be kind. "I am not going anywhere."

I ran downstairs and got Mac's screwdrivers and pliers, and a roll of throwaway paper (a sacrifice, which she never afterwards mentioned), and the turpentine. What I did, working carefully with a screwdriver and pliers, was to remove the toilet seat entirely. Mary was then able to waddle into the living room and lie on the floor, prone. With great caution I sort of diluted the enamel with the turps as she lay on her stomach, occasionally beating the floor or giving the rug a substantial chew.

After a while, I was able to release her from the encumbrance and clean off the paint. That sensitive Irish skin . . . her language was awful, and there *was* a largish pink ring.

When the job was finished, I applied an excellent burn ointment. She stayed as she was for a while. She'd been through a lot.

"I shall never forgive Mr. Swensen," Mary said. "Never. Never."

"Give it time; you'll forget."

"Never."

I thought she was unforgiving, but that was before Mr. Swensen varnished the front hall one night when Mac and I were involved.

We both looked into space, recovering.

Finally Mary said, "I wonder what the interns would think of *this?*"

A number of ideas came into my mind, but I doubted she'd appreciate them. I bit my lip.

"Go ahead," she said, "laugh."

I did.

3

I was thinking about dinner one morning when the phone rang. We had considered having the phone disconnected in order to save money, but had been told I would need it when school started and my roving assignments were scheduled. As soon as I answered, I knew it was bad news.

Mr. Hartford was the assistant superintendent of schools, and a professional nice guy. He was also a personal nice guy. The superintendent, Mr. Pawalton, was aloof, intelligent, and stern, although understanding. They seemed a planned combination; like the good detective and the mean detective.

"Hope I am not disturbing you," said Mr. Hartford cheerfully, disturbing me.

"Not at all."

"Well!"

Silence on my part, unless he could hear my heart pounding.

"Miss Rogers, I am sorry. . . ."

"Mrs. Macfarlane."

"Mrs. Macfarlane. You know the voters rejected the proposed school budget?"

"I read about it in the newspaper."

"Ah. You were part of the budget."

"I was?"

"Yes. It is with the greatest reluctance I must tell you there will be no place for you this fall."

"There won't?"

"No."

I didn't say anything. I couldn't.

"Miss . . . Mrs. Macfarlane?"

"Here."

"You do understand we have your name on file and the minute, the minute we get the go-ahead signal, we'll call. Right?"

"Thank you."

"I am very sure the people will recognize the positive necessity for more funds."

"Thank you."

"Thank *you*." I didn't know why we were thanking each other, unless it was for the absence of hysterics, which I was strongly considering having. I could tell he sensed my panic and disliked being the hatchet man. All I could think of was pots and pans, five dollars a week, my debt.

The company had warned us. Mr. J. C. Penney had had a horror of owing money; I'd read his book. There is no place for an extravagant fool in the retail business. I had been one. What if Mac got fired because he had married an extravagant fool, some kind of a nut, which I had tried to avoid being?

I had vowed I would be a good wife to Mac and not give in to vapors. There are times when the retail business is conducive to vapors, but one does not have them.

I gave in. I cried and cried. I'd just get stopped, then remember those miserable pots, and I'd start again. Went on all day. My eyes were bloodshot and my face puffy by five o'clock. I started wringing out cold cloths and draping them over my face, leaving a hole around my mouth for breathing and howling.

There was a knock on the door. I ignored it. Pretty soon the lock clicked and I heard someone come in. Too early for Mac, surely, but I nearly had a heart attack before I lifted a corner of a cloth and saw Mary. She was standing in the middle of the living room.

"Katie . . ."

"Yar," I moaned.

"Are you hurt?"

"Yar."

"Where?"

"In my head."

"Nothing can be that bad."

I groaned.

"Tell me."

I told her. The whole thing.

She agreed losing the job was sad, but not fatal. She was curious about the kitchen equipment, but I had a sort of fit at thinking of it, so she desisted

"I work at Sears, you know," Mary said.

We knew. We tried never to think of Sears. She rarely mentioned the company in our presence. She was only a reserve; we were career. Penneys was our lifeblood.

"One of my friends is quitting. Moving out of town."

"Best of British luck," I muttered.

"She's in sportswear. Covers in housewares part time."

"Housewares." I shuddered. Housewares I had.

"Know anything about sportswear?"

"Sports. My tennis is lousy and the golf instructor in school said I was the worst he had ever seen. I took posture all the way through the university. Hung from the posture bars for half an hour a day. Got credit."

"Shut up," said Mary. "You don't *play* *a*nything, you sell slacks and sweaters and stuff. And then, if they need help in housewares, you go to that department. Toasters and coffeepots . . ."

"Pots. Maybe I could sell mine to Sears, on the quiet."

"Use your head, Katie. Dear God, you try that and you'll end up in prison; maybe it's a federal offense. Did you ever work in a store?"

"I used to help out in Father's."

"Perfect," she beamed. "Look, you come in tomorrow."

Sears?

"I'd have to arrange my schedule to suit Mac's."

"It can be done, I think."

"Wouldn't there be a—a conflict of interest?"

"No. My father was with Sears; he's retired now, but his best friend was always the Penney manager."

"They were probably older and had mellowed through the years. Mac has not made a start on mellowing."

"You mean he hates Sears?"

"No. He loves Penneys."

Mac did. He liked his work and had a strong sense of loyalty. I knew he would prefer a different job for me, on general principles.

He will never know. Better for his peace of mind.

Then I gasped. "Which plaza?"

"Greenwood."

Thank heaven. Greenwood Mall had a Penney store, but it was not Mac's. His was at College Place Plaza. I could just go to Sears, do my best, and march home again, avoiding the Penney store in case I should meet someone who worked there.

"You'll have a discount."

I almost fainted. Sears label—Penney home.

"You come in tomorrow at ten; that's when they interview. I'll talk to Mr. Folger about you. He's in personnel. I can't promise, Katie; I'm only a flunky myself, but I honestly think you have a good chance if you're on the spot when Julia gives notice, especially when she's leaving right away. Her husband is army."

"Yar."

"By the way, don't go square, but avoid the Yip look, will you? Could you do your hair a little differently?"

There it was again; the hair business. "What difference does it make how I want to wear my hair?"

"Off the job, okay. But you have to be practical; most customers hate to find a hair in a display barbecue, for some reason. And if you lose a three-foot strand around a male shopper's coat button or on his shoulder, there's a possibility of a domestic encounter when he goes home."

"My hair doesn't fall out," I said, offended.

"Everyone's does. What brunette hausfrau wants to see her man with a blond hair anyplace about him? Huh?"

"I should take to a snood?"

"Don't be silly. *Try*, Katie. Try to be practical. Please?"

I was fenced in. "You tired at night?"

"Dead. But I never tell Bill; he'd use me for a case history. I only hope my legs and feet hold out until he passes the boards. Katie, it's fun in a store. There are the people, all kinds. And there is a special challenge, finding the right outfit or pan—sorry!—for them."

"Yar." The cold compress on my face slipped sideways. Mary removed my cloth arrangement and got some witch hazel and applied it, then put the cloths back on. I knew I'd look almost human any minute. I asked how her wound was.

"The turpentine made a kind of red circle," she said delicately. "Bill offered to pay me if I'd go to the clinic for diagnosis. I will not."

"You mean he'd use you for a guinea pig?"

"He likes to kid the interns. They'd never guess what caused it. Such an experience is not common. They wouldn't have a clue. You have a lot to learn about medical students, Katie. They absolutely zero in on wounds and difficulties. But the ones I know would never consider the dreadful trauma of being stuck to the toilet seat. They'd *laugh*."

"Was Bill really serious about the clinic?"

"I'm not sure. But I think he married me because my eyes are different colors. Fascinated him."

I removed the cloths, sat up. Checked her eyes. Sure enough. One was blue with brown specks, and one was brown with blue specks. I mean . . . well. . . . "I thought they were both blue."

She was pleased. "That's another thing. People see what they want to see; some think I have blue eyes, others think brown. Bill may write a paper on it someday."

I was appalled, but relieved at the same time. If you have something, doctors may be more interested in the thing than in you. Oh, sure, the best ones no doubt consider the entire patient, although I can think of times when I'd just as soon they did not. Viz., Mary's round rash.

"I'm going to lie down," said Mary. "These days I'm more comfortable lying or standing. Our bed is soft, and anyway, I'm so flopped that I'm apt to say to Bill when he comes home, 'The trouble with *you* is . . .'"

I nodded.

"That is a revolutionary tactic leading to violence," she sighed. "Psychiatrists are extremely complicated."

Hoping for a last-minute reprieve, I said, "You're sure I should come tomorrow?"

"Positive."

I made salmon loaf that night; a can of salmon can go a long way, especially when you load it with bread crumbs. I was absent-minded, thinking about Sears, and put in four eggs instead of two, so the loaf was on the custard side, but satisfactory.

Next morning I waved Mac off and dusted the baseboards like a maniac, moving with the speed of light. I got out some hamburger and left it on the drainboard to defrost. Then I chose a subdued orange and black dress, fastened my hair back with three barrettes and took the bus to Greenwood Mall. Found my way to personnel and sat for forty-five minutes, contemplating my future. It was as if I were invisible. Everyone was rushing around with sheaves of papers and going into huddles, and everyone knew what it was all about, except me. This situation would continue for some time, but I did not know that then. I would have left, but thought of my kitchen cupboards, loaded, and remained.

Just as I had concluded I was a ghost, the door to the inner sanctum opened and Mr. Folger beckoned to me. Neither Sears nor Penneys is a firm that employs hordes of secretaries with British accents, or carpets the execs' offices with ankle-deep rugs—more likely tile. Such frills add to costs, and anything that adds to costs is a capital crime. I am not fooling.

I went into the office and filled out a form, and Mr. Folger looked me over. I do mean *over*; I was to discover he was a pat-pat-patter, but pleasant. Among the men em-

68

ployees there were also bust peekers and waist watchers, and an ankle man or two. Legs seemed to receive the most attention. After all, the division managers were only human, and surrounded by women. Thoughts stray. I had never fully appreciated this, and nervously considered Mac at Penneys. One saving grace in a department store: there isn't much time for hanky-panky. Stair wells and small cubicles abound and are not off limits, but play opportunities are somewhat limited.

Mr. Folger and I talked for a while. As I was doing the demure bit, I developed a curiosity about the kind of toothpaste he used. He had the whitest choppers I'd ever seen. All his own, too. They did not go into a glass at night but probably gleamed throughout the dark hours, beacons for Mrs. Folger.

We discussed my schedule, and I mentioned one I could handle (when Mac was working, so I could get home before he did). We settled on a four-day week. A plaza operation is flexible, and since the store is open six nights a week, there is need for salespeople at varying times.

Mr. Folger asked if I could go to the three-hour orientation course, which was luckily being given at this moment; I had not missed more than a quarter of an hour. Fifteen minutes sounds more impressive when you say quarter of an hour.

I said I could join it immediately. Or sooner. Payments on the pots started in two weeks. Also, I was not at ease with Mr. Folger.

There is more to learn about a department store than a customer could possibly imagine. *I* could not imagine it, and I may have missed something just sitting there and appreciating all Mac had to put up with, but largely I concentrated. It was school. At one point, after asking a stupid question, I was afraid I might not graduate. I began to get slap-happy, and hoped we'd have caps and gowns when the course was over. Perhaps I would receive a diploma.

The time passed quickly, and then I went on the floor, selling. I realized how much I had needed those three hours, and was sorry I had been facetious about the training. I was lost, all right; if I could have remembered every single fact I had been told, there would have been less difficulty.

The rest of the day was a blur. Writing up a sale is complicated. I didn't know where everything was. Customers avoided me because they could see I was new, and I had to move in on them with determination. I may even have frightened a few, but I needed that job. I went into housewares when ordered, and almost immediately a little boy got his thumb caught in a waffle iron. We couldn't figure out how he managed to do it, but there it was. With his constant nerve-racking bellowing, he couldn't tell us, and come to think of it, how the thumb got *in* was not the problem. Getting it *out* was the problem. The division manager held the waffle iron, and the mother worked on the thumb, meanwhile threatening to (1) kill the kid, (2) sue the store. During this time, there was no one but me to serve the customers. I rang up three inaccurate sales on the cash register, and could not figure out how to ring up a twenty-two-cent sale at all. Something about twenty-two cents bugged me, I guess, for the principle was the same. Also, I had never known what a cash register could do to a sales person, physically. Twice, while I was trying to ring up a sale, the drawer came out and hit me in the stomach. The first time the little boy was making so much noise that no one could have heard me; actually I was incapable of sound because the breath was knocked out of me. I know I don't breathe through my stomach, but I quit all breathing whatsoever. It was awful. After that I was more careful, but it got me again when I was least expecting it, and the gentleman customer was no gentleman. He said, laughing, "Girl, you ought to wear a suit of armor." He then took his package and left.

Oh, the business world is hard. It is hard.

There were no seats left on the bus when I went home, but it didn't matter. I could feel nothing. I wobbled into the apartment, soaked my feet for fifteen minutes in the largest pot, took two aspirin, and pitched into dinner, which was on time. The hamburger was overdone, and that made Mac happy. I refrained from mentioning it was because cooking it so surely destroyed any bacteria that might have developed while it was defrosting during the long, long day. In fact, when I had arrived and seen the hamburger on the drainboard, it reminded me of me: perfectly limp.

After I waved Mac off to work for the evening (thinking how brave and gallant and noble he was), I collapsed on a cushion in the living room. I had to think.

Totaling up my experience, I found several pluses. I had not been bored. I had actively hated only two customers, was neutral toward three, and very much wanted to help the others. I mean, when a woman wants a grill for her mother who is eighty-four and lives in Muskegon and doesn't cook enough but would with the right kind of safe, electric grill—well, it was rewarding to discover we had just what she needed. On the other hand, when a woman is determined to buy a pants suit a size too small, with a jacket that doesn't cover her most outstanding feature, it is difficult; but one develops a philosophy. After the three-way mirror did not convince her the outfit was a terrible mistake, nothing more could be done. I wrapped it up.

Another plus. I found I cared. I truly wanted each person to look his best, or have what he could buy and wanted. I even discovered I could wait on two people at once, remembering individual needs, and it occurred to me that—someday—I might be able to work up to three or four customers simultaneously. Without making anyone mad, I mean. (Customers these days, the more experienced help told me, were unusually hostile.)

When Mac arrived home after Penneys closed that night, he watched TV while I napped, bolt upright. We went to bed. I ached all over at this point, and my subconscious did its best to betray me. Several times I sat up in bed and made firm statements, such as, "It's marked down" or "I'm afraid we don't have your size." I was more or less mumbling, the way you do when you're asleep and think you're speaking clearly and sensibly, so Mac didn't understand. After I had directed two customers to the ladies' rest room, he said I must have eaten something that upset me. I could have told him it was either the bacteria in the hamburger or Sears, but it was no time to start a rhubarb. Somehow my subconscious let up, and while I turned and tossed, my mouth no longer flapped.

When I woke the next morning, I knew at once something was wrong and quickly realized what it was. Waved Mac off, looked over the baseboards, and went to business. I shall always remember that morning because of two important facts: I still had my job at Sears, and henceforth and forever after I ignored baseboards, more or less.

On the bus I nearly panicked thinking about things to be signed for by the supervisor (this may be some older, experienced salesperson or division manager or merchandise superintendent), and I thought about charge slips, and sales slips, and people, and the murderous cash registers. By the time I arrived I had a case of stage fright, but I got over it in the frenzy that followed.

We had straightened up merchandise and done what we were supposed to, and the store opened, and a little girl dropped a box of popcorn right in front of me, on the floor. Buttered. Actually she should not have been eating popcorn at that hour. It scrunched and scattered on the tile, and I skidded around, and the division manager came with a helper to clean it up and said, "I hate the goddamn popcorn, and someday I am going to wreck Garfinkle's machine with a sledgehammer."

"I will bring a crowbar," I said, "and give a hand."

As time went on, I found out how a person could develop a hatred for popcorn. I, myself, will not touch another kernel. Well, maybe: unbuttered. I used to adore the stuff, and it grieved me to put away my yen, with other childish things.

Mary and I met for lunch in the employees' lunchroom. She was appalled when I took my sandwich out of my purse; peanut butter in perpetuity would not do. I told her about Mac and his feeling concerning cultures in meat, and she said he had a neurosis, which I must try to understand but, for myself, ignore. I explained about egg on the fork, and how Mac had been sick along with two hundred and fifty-three other people who ate custard pie at a church supper many years ago, and that there was also something about maggots, which he efused to divulge. I had not inquired because I thought it was war stuff.

Nonetheless, Mary said, I must have something other than peanut butter. After due consideration, I decided I would when I got tired of it. Not before.

73

Mary and I agreed that no one, absolutely no one at the apartment should know about my new job. Not even Mrs. Swensen. If I had to talk about it, Mary said, I should confide either in her or in Randolph. I had to have a reason for being gone so much, and we decided I wouldn't mention losing the job I never began: roving sub. If I couldn't think of enough to say about roving sub, then I could use diversion—such as Children's Hospital, where I was starting as an aide on Friday. We both knew that I usually could think of something to say; that had always been one of my main problems.

My schedule was: Mon., Tues., Weds., Thurs., staggered hours at Sears; Fri., Children's Hospital. The thought of Sat. was unsetting because what with washing, cooking, marketing, cleaning, when would I do the Novel?

The Novel would have to wait. Probably my reason for not working on the Novel was the same reason many other novels never got written. When I consider some I have read lately, that doesn't seem a bad idea.

From a distance, I once overheard some members of the jet set in Europe discussing what a beastly bore life in general was, and sex was, and the world was; and I did observe that most of the children (they weren't around very often) of these people were sort of mixed up as to who was who, and how related. So my Novel could wait in the wings. Anyway, all I had to write about was the common work life of ordinary people, who were trying—sometimes successfully, sometimes not—to make sense out of an unreasonable world. And probably no one wanted to hear about Sears and Penneys. I mean PENNEYS and Sears.

Oh, steady on.

Point is, Mac and I agreed we had to eat and the government, which was only us and others, couldn't possibly feed us all unless we did something useful. So we had to work and receive payment for such, which in turn went into food and clothing. And work was interesting; better than base-boards, which were probably only another way of playing with your toes. Our climate, moreover, was not conducive to grass skirts and conch shells. I knew about grass skirts, of course, but Mac told me of certain areas where men used conch shells for shorts. They would do better shopping at Sears.

Mac and I also agreed that the U.S. was a good place to live; when you lived in other places, there was always something wrong. I mean, more wrong than we have, which is plenty. Anyone could see by our schedules that we would never have time for political activity. We were in an election year, so we'd listen to the radio, read the newspaper (Mr. Swensen's), meet the candidate when possible (and if there was no charge), and make up our minds. We'd rather meet the candidate than listen to the radio or read the newspaper—or mags. There are jerks among writers and broadcasters; I often recognize the jerk in me but am hopeful it will lessen in a few years. Actually, Mac and I distrust instant information.

Then there's the matter of experience. We didn't have any. We were aware, all right, and we cheered for the guy on the white horse with the white hat, but it's hard to know what's what. Sometimes we found we'd cheered a merry-go-round horse and a candidate who was only after the brass ring. So we weren't going to change anything tomorrow, but the day after possibly, when we found out the facts.

What TV can do to a qualified but ugly (fat/skinny, in-articulate, horse-faced, piggy-eyed) office seeker is a shame. One needs personal contact. I mean, how is the guy, really? Could be fat/skinny, inarticulate, horse face, piggy eye *is* on a true white horse with a true white hat.

Mac's and my political problems were compounded because we belonged to different parties. We made a big thing out of voting for the *man* but noticed we usually went for the *man* in our own party. So we weren't objective. The best way to get over the almost impossible hurdle of different parties was to refuse to discuss the candidate. But we set up ground rules: first raised voice, no more discussion. First quietly *vicious* voice, no more. We stopped early in our arguments; we always started out cool and ended up hot.

We wanted to do the right thing, which meant right for others, too. In real life that is very difficult. We were political but opposed to anyone who argued with bombs, tire chains, knives, guns, or baseball bats (painted dark so they don't show on TV). Whose freedom are they buying?

Crazy.

Outside the political scene there were differences. Mac had a closed mind on the coming-up art show at The Gallery, and Sue, Whuffor, Bill, and Mary were not enthusiastic either. I coaxed and coaxed. I said that (1) this was a preview and special; I was invited and could bring guests— them; (2) marvelous artists were exhibiting; (3) the exhibit was big, tri-city, so there was much to see; (4) the show was *free*. This last argument helped me win. Also, it would be on a Sunday afternoon, and we all had the day off.

I hadn't truly triumphed, however, until the day came. It was beautiful: sunny, crisp, with a hint of autumn gold. We couldn't stay home; even an art show was better than nothing, they all agreed. We would go in the Campagna's car. It was the biggest.

At the last minute, we invited the Swensens. They hardly ever went anywhere. It was crowded and we overlapped, but we drove happily off, with Randolph protecting the back door of the apartment. If it had been permitted, we would have included Randolph.

Mr. Swensen said afterwards he'd had his outing for the year; maybe for the rest of his life.

Parking was difficult at The Gallery, but not half as bad as the football games or the Penney parking lot; so I don't know why everyone fussed so. Mary's feet were hurting before we finished the brief walk to the place, and so were mine, but at least I kept quiet about it. In one of Mac's sports magazines I had read about how boxers soak their hands in some solution to harden them, and I decided I'd try the same stuff for my arches.

When we got to the courtyard, there were all sorts of sculptures, some with those fascinating holes clear through them, and at that point we lost Mr. Swensen.

We had only just missed him when we heard, "Yah, Sharlie!" and turned to find he had climbed a sculpture and had poked his head through the top hole, about twelve feet off the ground. His pipe was sending out clouds of pollution. He viewed the rest of us beatifically; as a matter of fact, his expression was asinine.

I was really angry. I said, "Come down at once!"

Mr. Swensen just grinned and removed his pipe by reaching around the outside of the sculpture hole. "Yust the thing," he said, "for Randolph."

Whuffor sat down on a lovely marble egg (standing on end and beautifully veined) and laughed so hard he fell off. Bill and Mac clutched each other and roared like fools.

"Don't be vulgar," I yelled furiously.

Mrs. Swensen was so upset she got back her Scandinavian accent. "Mister, you vill fall and break. Ah, Mister . . ." She always called him that.

Sue and Mary were suddenly attacked by laughter, and

right then a man came rushing up shouting for Mr. Swensen to get *down.*

"Ay vont to," he said, simply. "Ay don't know how."

"How in hell did you get up there?" shouted the man, in a fury.

"Ay vill always vonder," said Mr. Swensen.

That got me, and I sat on the ground and roared, along with the rest. We were a disgrace, and knew it. We could not help it.

Bill and Mac pulled themselves together (Whuffor was useless), and they went back and guided Mr. Swensen's feet into the holes so he could descend. Smoke was coming from all the holes as he went past them with that rotten pipe. The attendant turned out to be the sculptor, and prizes were being awarded. Prizes never go to amusing things, everything is so serious these days; the smoke holes got to the judging committee, but naturally they couldn't pin (stick? tie?) an award ribbon on anything so funny.

We were a more subdued group as we went up the side steps into The Gallery, and I was grateful for that because I was afraid we would not be admitted after our fiasco in the courtyard.

In the vestibule of The Gallery there were tremendous structural steel and iron exhibits. Sue was fascinated with one that had cogs, wheels, and what resembled (and were, I think) bicycle handle bars. The apex was a small church steeple. Sue walked around it again and again while we were looking at other pieces, and when we ventured on, we discovered she was missing, so we had to go back. We knew we all had to stay together or we'd be lost forever. She was still going around the structure, sort of hypnotized.

Whuffor took her arm, gently. "Come on, darling."

"But Romeo, don't you see?"

More people had arrived, and they stared at Romeo and Sue.

"See what?" He was irritated; he hated to be stared at or called Romeo.

"It will never work," said Sue. "Never in a million years!"

"You are so right," crowed Bill, and he took Sue's other arm and he and Whuffor led her away. She hardly noticed Bill, because she was having a serious argument with Whuffor.

We walked on. I devoutly wished we had never come, but hoped the worst was over. At this point, we were in the wood-carving room, and that seemed safe; but Mac wanted to know what everything *was*, and some *weren't*.

There was a figure titled *Woman—Fecundity*. It was about twenty feet high, and was made like those little Oriental carved-ivory balls—you know, one inside the other, until there is just a wee speck. Inside each figure in this carving, cut so you could see, was another figure, and inside *that*, another—until you came to a sort of gnome, absolutely obscene for some reason.

Mary looked and looked, studying it.

Then she quietly threw up.

Bill and Mac and Whuffor guided Mary to a stone bench, where she recovered, although she lost ground when she discovered she was sitting on a sarcophagus. There was a printed sign, a translation, I imagine. It said: *What I gave away, I have.* Mary pondered on that, and while it wasn't the most cheerful message in the world, it was thought-provoking and took her mind off her stomach.

Sue and I got paper towels from the nearby ladies' room and cleaned up the floor. Momentarily, I felt sorry for myself; I was always cleaning something. Finished, we joined the group, Mary apologized to whoever or whatever was in the ancient coffin (for sitting on him), and we started on.

The Swensens were missing.

We scurried around and were about to check at Lost and Found when we heard an argument in the next gallery. It had a Scandinavian sound, so we advanced toward it. There was a mirrored room in one unit—I mean, it was a room within the gallery with ropes around it, and a little path leading into it. In order to enter the mirrored room, one had to remove one's shoes. We later discovered Mr. Swensen had a hole in his sock, and Mrs. was so mortified she wanted him to put his shoes back on. He would not, and went into the unit. She remained outside, but saw us coming, quickly removed her shoes and went in. We could all hear Mr. Swensen's "Yah, Sharlie!" He just kept saying it, enthralled. Only one person at a time was permitted to enter, and an attendant was informing them that one must come out. I felt if he had been around when they went in, and he was supposed to be guarding the place, we wouldn't have been in this situation. Mrs. Swensen answered him by giggling, and Mr. Swensen was saying "Yah, Sharlie!" It sounded like the classic chase, and even Bill was horrified. Psychiatrists are not supposed to be horrified at anything, so he was out of character. In fact, everyone was but me. I was on the verge of something.

The attendant sat down on the floor and began untying his—well, they seemed to be moccasins, although I had never seen them tied like that. Probably his own design. However, he was spared undoing all the knots because the Swensens emerged right then. They didn't hear the tirade they got from the moccasin man. They were so sort of cute that even his fury fizzled out. Mrs. Swensen's cheeks were much pinker than usual, and every once in a while Mister would give her a small dig in the ribs, and she'd giggle some more.

"All mirrors," said Mr. Swensen. "Yah, Sharlie."

"Yah," said Mrs. Swensen. "Whoever heard such?"

The rest of us entered, singly and at proper intervals. The floor was a mirror, the ceiling and walls were mirrors, chair, table—all constructed of mirrors, no visible framing. I didn't understand what had amused the Swensens so, and there was no use asking. Maybe Mister was a pantie peeper. Though I had not been in the business world very long, I was becoming cynical.

It was a great relief when we went into the gallery where all the paintings were. There was something for everyone, and no possibility of a mishap. We thought Bill had fallen in love with the subject of one portrait; she had three eyes and that was the sort of thing to interest him. But he told us what really fascinated him was what the painter thought, and what the subject thought. It all got terribly complicated; we left him to his own and other's thoughts.

In the big gallery of paintings we could scatter; it was enormous. But everything was in plain sight. Reminded me a little of the long room at Versailles. We agreed to meet each other in an hour at the other end. So the couples strolled around, running across one another from time to time. Mac was greatly taken with a scene that had an indefinable something. It was called *In the Forests,* and I mentioned those four lines of William Blake's: "Tiger! Tiger! burning bright/In the forests of the night,/What immortal hand or eye/Could frame thy fearful symmetry?"

Mac didn't ask me what the meaning was; I didn't know, anyway. I liked them. So did he. The painting was strange: way back in the mists of it there was a figure—or was it? A man? A woman?

I would have thought it the last thing in the world to appeal to Mac, and I was shaken because I didn't know him. Not all the way. Not after our time together, and love.

I felt threatened; in an odd fashion, the painting was threatening, too. Not the figure—or was it?—but the darkness and mists, the depths. We stayed a long time.

"William Blake was different," I said.

"So is this painter." Mac was intent.

"Yes. Blake said, 'To see a world in a grain of sand/And a heaven in a wild flower,/Hold infinity in the palm of your hand/And eternity in an hour.'"

"Sure," said Mac. But he liked Blake, as well as the painting.

We went on, then; and I would never forget the Mac who was unknown to me. I was suddenly sick of myself and my pretensions, and of others like me. *We* understand, *we* suffer, *we* speak, *we* have empathy. Inward-looking, we move in the narrow rut of self. Empathy? Echoes . . .

I was reminded of an incident at dinner in the home of a prof who was a sociologist when I was in school.

During the dinner, a man said, "We ought to have more empathy."

Someone laughed. "But not for clods."

Another guest said, "Define empathy."

Define it, define it, define it. You don't define it; you have it.

That evening I became somewhat anti-intellectual; I mean, anti-smart-aleck intelligent, not the real kind.

At strategic points in the long gallery were marble statues, and we observed Sue circling one. Then we noticed that the marble nymph resembled Sue, in shape and smiling attitude. It was funny and she was pleased, not upset the way she had been with the steelworks.

We saw the Swensens waiting at the far door and, converging, Mary and Bill. We went toward them.

"Step outside, and I'll tell you what I mean, you bastard."

We turned and saw Whuffor. He was so enraged he could hardly speak, and that was no doubt fortunate. He was facing a man who was about the same size—taller and more slender, perhaps—and blond. Also, supercilious.

"I paint as I like."

"And I think what I want to. Damn fool. Okay?"

"*Not* okay." The painter was no coward.

Whuffor stepped forward. "You hang it up, you stick out your neck. Chop. You get my opinion. I gotta *bow*?"

"I'll continue to express myself."

"I don't like the painting. I don't like you. I've expressed myself."

There was going to be a fight.

Fortunately then, right then, a girl rushed up and threw her arms around the artist. "Darling, you're made! Tonio is going to write you up; come on, he's waiting."

Sue hurried to Whuffor—I hadn't seen when she left her marble twin—and clasped hands with him. "Hey—*there* are the Swensens."

They were there, all right. We all were, and we went out and sat on the wide terrace and watched and thought and talked a little, not much. The sun was low on the horizon, turning the clouds pink and gold and mauve, and before us was the most remarkable artistry of all. I remembered Blake's "If the sun and moon should doubt,/they'd immediately go out."

We were all tired and happy and puzzled and wondering. When we got back to the apartment, Randolph was waiting, and he greeted each of us with great enthusiasm, being a diplomat.

I heard the phone ringing in our apartment, and that's usually when you can't get there in time, but Mac is fast with the key, so I made it before they hung up.

It was the director of volunteers at Children's Hospital. The volunteer quota was filled, she said.

I leaned against the wall and thought, Here we go again. "I'm sorry."

"So am I," she said, "but we have another job for you, Mrs. Macfarlane. There is such a need. If only . . ."

"If only what?"

"We're desperate," she said. "No one really wants to go there, and the need is so great. . . ."

"What?" I was impatient.

"State Hospital," she blurted. "The women's ward; locked ward. We've looked over your qualifications and you've had psychology and sociology—enough for volunteer needs. And I know you have compassion. Please, Mrs. Macfarlane, do help us to give them a chance."

I thought dully I'd have no children to love or comfort. I knew I received love and comfort in return from the little ones, and I needed something extra. Now this. I guess I had it figured too easily; that wasn't enough to do for Eric —something harder. This was.

And Eric had had everything to give. And he was gone.

I said, "To whom do I report?"

She was stunned for a moment, and then there was a lot more guff, but I kept on thinking of Eric, and I knew the director of volunteers. She was all right; if she said I should go, I should.

I was to report Friday at eight to Dr. Kasmir Kintosky, State Hospital.

4

Among the questions Mr. Folger had asked, off-handedly, was whether I believed I could work well with women. I said *yes*. I like human beings, basically; not all of them, and not all the time, but women are human beings and so are men, and hurrah. However, one Thursday a charming gentleman came shopping, visited and talked and bought a key purse for his little girl. I developed a reaction to charming gentlemen after that—I gave him change for ten dollars instead of the five dollars he had given me because he kept mentioning the ten dollars he had given me, and he also told me about exercises to do for ski knee, which I did not have and probably never would. My skiing is on a par with my tennis.

When the register was short that afternoon, I had a sort of illumination and described the pleasant customer. Mr. York, the division manager, looked grim and said everyone knew him, yes, they did. He warned me *again* about putting cash from the customer on top of the cash drawer and making change with it in plain sight. I had been conned by a shortchange artist. Artist. I felt like Whuffor when he was going to sock the painter. I mean, Whuffor had explained afterwards he was convinced the artist racket had gone too far; the artist figured, he, Whuffor, was so stupid he, Whuffor, did not recognize that a blob of paint was a blob of paint. We agreed writers had gone too far, too. The artist and/or writer can become a con man.

I was so angry at the crook, and so furious over being tricked, I was murderous. I truly was; I wanted to kill him. Oh, the jerk. My only consolation (slight) was that he was one of the top professionals.

Naturally, I was afraid I would be fired, as well as have to refund the money to Sears, which would be a switch, but Mr. York said this sort of thing could happen, although it would be best to let it happen *once*. He told me I did not have to give him $8.70 from my own purse. What a break; I did not have $8.70. Mr. Clift had just collected for the pots.

There is no describing how grateful I was to Mr. York, and how much I despised the thief. Probably his knee exercises would have crippled me for life. One feels soiled by an experience like that.

I was so serious and intense for several days that Mr. York said, "Look, sooner or later in our lives we meet con men of various kinds. You connected with one early in the game. Now you know. Tuck that knowledge away for future reference, Mrs. Macfarlane; I am sure you'll find use for it again, someday."

Naturally, the salesgirls were told, and they sympathized. They also explained about the checkers who came through the store occasionally to see if money was being taken by employees from the registers without having been rung up, which was stealing. I felt as Mac did. I was developing a loyalty to the store, and the way Mr. York had been so decent, though grim, made me feel fortunate to work for Sears. I wondered if I might become all mixed up, playing on Mac's opposing team, as it were. I decided, though, that appreciation that seemed to be developing into affection was all right. In my own area, I had a right to respond. I was dismayed I'd been taken, but I'd make it up to Sears, somehow.

That is the way I felt, and if it sounds like corn, okay. (Not popcorn.)

Then I saw some young children swinging on the bathrobe display. I think I was in the manic phase at that point; the depression was over, although it seems to me manic-depressive feelings sweep throughout a department on some days. You get so you can't stand to miss another sale, not *one* more. I went over, told the children, grinding my teeth, to stop ruining the robes, and they scurried back to their mothers. I would even have tangled with a tiger mother at that point. I often seemed to be a combination policeman-physician-mother-father and, mostly, Sympathetic Ear. Sympathetic Ear sells merchandise. People have troubles, and they will tell them to the salesperson. You have to be born with an Ear; there's no faking it. I am their confidante on the park bench. Though I had been working a short time, the regulars started coming back, and I became acquainted via the Ear with their entire families. It was gratifying; and some were pure Rapunzel. Like the day the woman told me her son was on hard drugs, and she talked and talked and cried, and bought a lime-tinted scarf, and decided to take him to the treatment center at the county hospital. I hardly said a word. She made the decisions. I hoped the lime scarf would bring her luck; it looked like a dream on her. She had mahogany-colored hair and freckles. Probably the shopping was therapy, because she made both decisions at the same moment. But I never found how it all came *out*, and that was unbearable.

In a way, women are more fun to sell to than men because they search and can't make up their minds and leave and come back, or bring a friend to help. Cotton briefs: polka dots, or stripes? It's exciting. One just never knows. Men arrive, buy what they want, and disappear. Unless they make a pass, which ends in everyone's disillusionment. I didn't get as many passes as Mary or Sue. Third on the totem pole. Men are easy, though.

Except when one shortchanges you. Oh, that poop.

Friday. I had told Mac about the change from Children's Hospital, and he said as long as State was not considered dangerous—all right. But why was the door locked?

An interesting question.

While I was telling Mac about State Hospital, I had heart pain. It wasn't anything I had eaten, I knew that. It was because I realized I could not continue to deceive him about Sears. I could not bear either to quit Sears or to tell him, and there were all those pans and Mr. Clift and everything. How ever and where ever could I confess? I was sure that even a good marriage, and ours was better and more wonderful than good, could not stand on shifting sands.

Deceit. How would *I* feel if Mac deceived me?

I thought, Surely there will be a moment, the unique moment, to tell him. Moreover, it would be far better for me to do it before anyone else did. News travels quickly in a small town, but in a city it also travels; there are those incredible coincidences. I could not delay too long.

But I had to wait for *when*.

I had made a sign for my room at school: I'M CAPRICORN. I WORRY.

I am. I do.

So then it was Fri.

Because of my university psych. and soc. studies, the indoctrination course was not required; but I sat in for an hour or two and reported back to the nurses' station: Ward AB. All was quiet behind the locked door, which, by the way, looked like the prison shakedown door I had seen on a soc. tour. Resembled the entrance to a vault.

Perhaps it was.

There was a push button beside the door, inside, if I needed to get out. What did they mean, *needed* to get out?

Oh, steady on. I wanted to go to the bathroom immediately, but repressed the urge. It was only fright.

The charge nurse gave me cards to read concerning the patients; that is, the barest minimum—name, age, birthplace, husband, children. More detailed files were confidential.

Then I was handed a basket and a bolt of cotton material, and told to teach the patients how to sew. Or, work with them, or whatever.

Sew. We were to make bedpan covers.

Burdened by basket and fabric, I was escorted into the locked ward by the attending psychiatrist and the charge nurse. I felt like a patient, and when I saw the patients, I felt even more so. They looked like me; some prettier, some not, some older, a few younger. I thought, Ohmygod, I will never make it out of here, and how will they know I'm *me* when this is over? A mistake could be made very easily. As far as I could see, the women around looked more normal than I did, whatever normal is.

"Do you have identification for me?" I asked the nurse.

"No. We don't like uniforms here, and we don't need identification. Most of our members, Mrs. Macfarlane, are almost ready to go back into the world."

"The hell with the world," said one. "You think we're nuts?"

We all laughed, but I thought she had something there.

"Mrs. Macfarlane has come to help you make bedpan covers," said the attending psychiatrist. Then he introduced me to each one, with an avuncular air, first-name basis . . . *me, Katie.* He did not look like any uncle I ever knew. The doctor and the nurse left quietly and quickly, something I had in mind, also.

I put my basket down on a long table, and thought guiltily of my bonus (for the pots and pans) sewing machine that was resting in the closet at home under a pile of books.

"Handmade bedpan covers," said a patient (member). "Will we embroider them?"

More laughter.

"We can decide," I said. "When I was in the hospital (tonsils), I bet I'd have felt better if the bedpan covers had daffodils or daisies or a Raggedy Ann on them. I suppose I sound silly."

"Do not be concerned about sounding silly around us," said a member. "We are experts."

"Once the embroidery gets in the chlorine wash, whammo! No color," said another.

I was concentrating on names; trying to remember everyone's. I knew it was important.

"Oh, yuh." I shook my head. "Suppose it does fade white. There's still a design. And suppose we made someone, somewhere in this hospital, know we care."

"Care. Sure."

I didn't know who said that; the words were like a sigh.

"When we finish the preliminaries, we'll take a vote," I announced brightly.

"I refuse to work on any bedpan cover in any way whatsoever." The speaker was lean and elegant and disdainful. Angie. She was fifty-eight, her card stated, but she looked much younger.

A woman who resembled a world's lady weight-lifting champion stood with arms akimbo on bulging hips. Slem was her name. She said a number of unprintable things about beds, pans, covers, and other women, including me.

"Oh, keep quiet." I was cross. "That's kid stuff; kid words. Now, please give me a hand with this material and we'll sit around the table."

To my surprise, they helped. I guess there wasn't anything more interesting to do. Angie put her nose in the air and went over and sat on the bench in the corner. When she said no bedpan covers, she meant no bedpan covers. Lucy, Slem, Alice, Edith, Jane, two Jeans (blue jeans?), Barbara, and me, Katie. That was the crew.

Out of the corner of my eye, I kept seeing Angie, alone.

From the basket, I took pins and needles (all counted twice over at the nurses' station before I came in, by me) and three pairs of scissors plus two measuring tapes. "Oh, this is a magic basket," I said, and despite the tan linoleum floor and three benches, long, heavy—making them harder to throw—and the bare table, I felt more cheerful. Although nervous. Slem could pick up a bench with one hand, I was sure, and use it for a battering-ram. Had the attending psychiatrist ever considered that? Probably not. Would anybody's uncle consider it?

Everyone stood around and watched me try to pull two benches to the table. "What's the matter?" I asked. "You underpaid?" So as I was huffing, Slem pulled up the other bench, one-handed. I thought so.

"Weak as a kitten," she grinned. "I've had too much shock."

Oh, steady on.

"Don't hand me that. If you put your mind to it, you could carry the table."

"I busted six fuzz, coming in," she admitted, proudly. "It was the seventh got me."

"Seven in one blow," said Angie, from the corner.

"You mind your own business," I told her. "Remember, you are not co-operating."

She turned her face to the wall. Anguished, I wondered if I'd set her back for six months. But they had warned me not to take any guff, and to act normally. That was what I was doing.

I sat down.

Everybody sat down, expectantly. Struck me as so damned pathetic, I had to examine the bolt of material until my eyes stopped watering. I didn't fool anyone.

"What's a nice girl like you doing in a place like this?" asked Jane. I thought it was Jane, anyway, and hoped before the session was over I would know who was who.

"I don't know." I put my elbows on the table, rested my face on my palms. "I can't sew."

"What do you mean, you can't sew?"

"Once, in home ec I had to take out a French seam, from a dish towel, mind you, five times."

"Well, for heaven's sake, Katie." Angie got up from the bench and came over to scrutinize me. "The least you can do is act like a social worker."

"I am not a social worker," I confessed, miserably.

"What're you good for, then?" Lucy spoke for the first time.

"I dunno. I'm supposed to be your helper or your friend. They can't get volunteers."

"No," said one of the Jeans. "Not under seventy. Everybody else is marching."

"Maybe they'll improve conditions," I said.

"Too late," said Lucy. "Well, you can try, at least."

"Where were *you* when the doctor said that?" Angie was, to my astonishment, defending me.

"So you're here for two hours." Alice spoke in singsong tones. "Poor, poor girl. Why do you bother?"

"Because of my brother." I told them about Eric. All about Eric.

"This is sure no kid's ward," said Slem. "Your brother'll be disappointed."

"God's children," Alice sang. "We're God's children."

I couldn't say anything at all. I mean, I couldn't. Finally I pulled myself together snappily. "Bless you."

"Maybe he's well out of it." Barbara looked down at her scarred wrists. "I mean, if it had to be. Someone like that— if I could have met him. . . ." I would remember Barbara always for her husky, lovely voice.

"Sure," said Slem. "You woulda had *him* in the locked ward."

"Let's get started," said the other Jean.

I looked in the basket. Nothing. "I think I've lost the pattern."

"You are really a dumb, stupid kid," said Slem. "Y'know, if you can make it outside, I sure ought to be able to."

"Yuh," I said. "Wait until I tell you what happened to me on my job yesterday. A con man . . ."

"Where you work?"—Jane.

"Sears."

"He saw you for a sucker, fast," she told me. "I used to con, sometimes. But it's really somethin' at Penneys; they've got this fool fuzz who doesn't look like anything at all, an' . . ."

"She's my friend," I said firmly. "So kindly refrain. Fact

93

is, though, I don't know what she looks like, either. Now I'm getting all of *you* sorted out, but I can never recall her. It's eerie."

"Face worth a fortune," Jane said. "I could of used it."

"If we don't get going," Alice, singsong, "Katie won't be allowed back here. Staff says useful activity. What staff says, we do."

I was baffled; by everything. Looking around the long table, I recognized the varying degrees of education and tradition. Each one had reached a breaking point.

At that moment, Edith who had not yet said a word, reached over, unfolded the fabric, and found the pattern neatly tucked inside.

"There it is; wow, are they ever organized. I love you, Edith." She didn't answer.

"Organized pandemonium. An accomplishment, indeed." —Angie.

"We'll cut a pattern *from* the pattern." I did it, glowing with confidence.

We all stared at the bedpan cover; something was wrong. It seemed small.

"You didn't leave room for the hem," sang Alice. "Oh, Katie."

I was crushed. "What'll we *do?* They count everything." The crew was amused; tickled, really.

"They'll never ask me to come again."

Angie reached over and patted my hand. "Never mind, dear. I'll work, too. I'll make a bib for my baby. He's seven months old." Triumphantly—"And I'll embroider it."

A bib for Angie's baby, seven months old. Her card had stated three grown children. *Where was Angie's baby?*

Ohmygod, I would have to ring the bell. Get out. I couldn't. I couldn't breathe. I was so sorry, so sorry.

"Come on, girls, get whackin'," said Slem.

We got whackin'.

Having made an error, I was not allowed to cut the material; I was permitted to hem, only. Some of what I hemmed, I was told to take out and do over. Barbara thought my work satisfactory, but no one else did.

On the bench in the corner, Angie was making the bib; I went over and marveled at the fine stitches.

"I was convent-trained," Angie said. "We were taught how to be gentlewomen."

"Some of the words I've heard you use"—Lucy—"did not come from any convent."

Hastily I explained, "My home-ec teacher tried with me."

"Not enough." Crisply. Angie made more fine stitches. "You can do anything you want to do. If you want to enough."

I found Angie highly irritating right then.

She grasped my wrist, with feather touch. "I don't have a baby," she whispered. "Sometimes I think I do because when Lawrence was six weeks old, we went to a dinner party. Most important. And he . . . he . . . Lawrence . . . And I keep thinking I must go home to him before he suffocates again. But he already did, you know."

"Never mind." Emotionally, talking with Angie was like swinging on a trapeze.

I went back to the hemming, and was moving right along when Edith said, softly, "My dear, it will not do. It really will not."

Everyone stared at Edith.

"It will, too," I said crossly. "These are only bedpan covers."

"Everything must be perfect."

"This is *my* best." I was stubborn.

One of the Jeans pinched me under the table. I didn't know what it was all about, but I subsided.

The group started talking again. We sounded like a Ladies Auxiliary, and under cover of the conversation, Jean explained that Edith *never* spoke.

"She just did," I pointed out.

It was difficult for me to accomplish much hemming; someone was always looking over my shoulder and suggesting I hold my needle differently, or that I should take smaller stitches.

I said, "You are driving me crazy."

We thought that was funny, but kept on working. When a bell went off with a great clang, I nearly hit the ceiling.

"The session is over," said Slem. She went unprintable again.

"You stop the kid stuff," I said.

"Baby, where I come from we learned that in our cradle, if we had one."

"Tough," I said. "Just too tough. Well, you talk like that and you get some other baby. Not me."

"Hoity-toity." But her heart wasn't in it.

"Sure. Now, shush; I have to count my supplies."

The pins came out right, and the scissors, and the tape measures. Put them in the basket.

I was one needle short. I know I blanched. "I have lost a needle."

The group examined each other; one or two slyly, I thought.

"We have to find it."

"Count again." Alice sang one-two-three-four-five-six-seven-eight-nine with me.

Still one short.

I got down on my hands and knees, and so did the others. We felt around on the floor and scanned it. As I was under the table, a needle fell beside me.

96

The door clicked and the charge nurse came. "What in the world . . .?"

I said, "I dropped a needle."

"Really, Mrs. Macfarlane; we're very particular about the sewing materials."

"I know." I was humble, as I should have been—penalty for carelessness. I knew only too well the weapon a needle could be—used either against one's self or someone else.

The session had lasted two hours. I was exhausted. It was harder than Sears; worse than the baseboards; more difficult than being pleasant and forgiving to Mr. Clift; more surprising than a small pat-pat from Mr. Folger, who had this tendency. He wasn't a nasty man; he needed to touch.

I carried the basket to the door. "Good-by, ladies," I said, and started singing it—the song.

"You'll come back, won't you?" asked Lucy.

I had to be honest. "I don't know."

"You hate us?"

"No. But it ruins my ego when everyone can do so much better than I can."

Unprintable, said Slem.

"Slem!"

"Well, my God, that's why we're here. Ruined insides. Dontcha see you give us hope?"

"What do you think failure does to me, huh? You think Katie Macfarlane is an iron woman? I've got feelings, too."

"You can cope," said Angie, lofty as usual. "You can or you wouldn't be stepping through that." She pointed at the door, locked even after the nurse had come in.

"Of course, Mrs. Macfarlane will return." The nurse took my arm. "She's volunteered."

"You can't let Eric down"—Barbara—"just because you don't like us."

"I do like you. Oh, all right. You win. I will practice stitching, you hear? See you next Friday, much improved."

Edith nodded. "We hope so."

The nurse's eyebrows went right up into her hairline, because Edith never spoke.

I left, but part of me was in the locked ward. Part of me will always be. Although the cast changes from time to time—people get well—the atmosphere remains the same. So does my sewing.

"Good therapy," said Dr. Kasmir Kintosky, when I reported to him.

"For whom?"

"For the patients," he said callously. "Who else? That's what we think here—everything for the good of the patient."

It was true. Understaffed, overcrowded, old; under constant financial pressure—they tried, and kept on trying. They did think of the patient.

They even thought of me. Until noon I was sitting in on indoctrination, getting supplies for the locked ward, working there, and reporting all that had happened to the psychiatrist. In the afternoon, I worked in the Auxiliary Gift Shop. It was not as busy as Sears, and we were supposed to be helpful rather than make a sale. When I found myself making a big pitch for a watering can to a ratfink who had come to see if his father was dead yet, I knew Sears had gotten to me. I closed my mouth and strolled to another counter. Ratfink thought his male beauty had affected me, and tried to get me back. I sent another girl.

The day had been too complicated. I hardly had time to eat dinner (quick chops) because I was telling Mac about State.

He said he'd watch for aberrations and oddities, and when he spotted them, he'd know what to do.

I narrowed my eyes. "I shall do the same for you. That habit you have of straightening your tie . . ."

He straightened his tie.

"Could be a highway to State. You are obsessive-compulsive. You do know that all the—uh—members are like us, only in many cases more sensible?"

We were about to debate further when there was a knock on the door.

It was Whuffor, out of breath and groaning under the weight of two big boxes.

"What?" Mac asked.

"Grapes."

"Grapes?"

"Ain't coconuts." Whuffor put the boxes on the floor by the counter.

"We don't want them." Mac picked up the grapes and staggered toward the door.

"As vice-president of Joy-Ever Wine Co., Inc., you have to accept the merchandise," said Whuffor.

"Whoever said . . . ? *Wine*. Well, so." Mac licked his lips, reflecting.

"Bacchus! We'll have a festival. Sue and Mary and I, Bacchae."

"Me Tarzan."

"A great idea, Whuff," said Mac.

It *was* great, except—"I'm not sure about making wine."

"It is mentioned frequently in the Bible," said Whuff. And that was so, I knew.

"Who's president?" Mac was suspicious.

Whuff bowed. "Me. You're vice; Bill is treasurer."

I wondered out loud what the Swensens would think.

"Mister is head taster," said Whuff.

We were in business, practically.

"The trouble *is*," added Whuff, not as decisive as usual, "these are table grapes. They are not wine grapes; most wine grapes are not sold for the table. They are usually too small and have too many pips; also, tough skins."

Mac sighed. "You have the organization, but no proper ingredients."

"Mother made some grape juice, once, that fermented," I said. "My father reported it was terrible grape juice, and poorer wine. But I drank some and got"—I grinned—"a small bun on."

"You what?" Whuff's big brown eyes rounded.

"I got a small bun on."

"She means," said Mac, crudely, "she got drunk."

"Not at all. A small bun is a small high. It was enough. Getting 'a small bun on' is my mother's term. She does *not* approve of it."

"Sounds kinda oldish," said Whuff.

We thought.

"I have to go on a trip for the firm. Leave tomorrow." Whuff meant he was taking the ancient truck and hawking vegetables down the coast; his father insisted on the experience—only thing that counted, he swore. "Be gone about five days. By the time I come back, it will be all over for those grapes. Say, I've got a cousin. . . ."

"No." Mac said, and I silently agreed. Whuffor had some odd relatives, and while that lot is common to us all, he had *more* than anyone we ever met. "While you're gone, Whuff, we'll make juice."

"No vats." Whuff was gloomy, after his enthusiastic start. He almost always acted before he thought, and that was probably why his father was so insistent.

"What *I* have"—I was impressive because I was telling the absolute truth—"is more pots and pans than you could ever imagine."

"So I heard." Whuff smiled. "But do you have a sixty-gallon container?"

"No," said Mac. "And thank God for that. Clift must have overlooked it. Now, friend, just leave it all to us."

"Yuh." Whuffor looked dubious. Suddenly he held out his hand to Mac, then to me. We shook hands all around; a contract.

The minute Whuffor left, Mac opened a box. When he lifted the top, a rich aroma escaped.

"These grapes are on the verge," he said.

"Of what?"

"Spoiling. We'll have to do them tonight."

I was so *tired*. "Maybe they should spoil a little?"

"Not *yet*. We must have a controlled operation."

"And the grapes are in control. Fine world; typical."

"No. We'll get the group in the apartment together. We'll all help. Many hands . . ."

"Blah, blah. You know Whuff won't help; he's going away tomorrow."

"He will help. I am going away, too."

"You?"

"To work. If I can, he can."

Me, too, I thought. Mac went and gathered the clan.

So we started boiling down the grapes, stupid happy. Since I was the only one with experience, except for Whuffor's cousin, I was in charge of boiling. But Sue and Mary and Mac and Bill and Whuff were right in there, picking off the grapes, washing (toxic spray?) and helping all the way. The kitchen became colorful; more purple than rose, and not true red burgundy, either. Even the dishcloth was stained.

"The Greeks wrote about this," I said. "Homer did. Odysseus got Cyclops drunk on wine."

"So what happened then?" Mary wanted to know.

"Cyclops passed out; a fortunate thing. He ate people."

"Mac," said Whuff, "this girl knows too much." He turned to me. "What year? I never heard about it."

"Probably around three thousand years ago; I'm not certain, really."

"That's what I like about you, Katie." Whuff wiggled his ears. "Right up to date."

"Nothing new about making wine," I said, scoring a point.

Mary had donated a pillowcase for straining.

"We have to watch out for the must," said Bill.

"Must what?"

"Dunno, exactly. I think must is the residue."

We looked up *must.* Dictionary said it was the expressed juice of the grape, or other fruit, before fermentation, or any juice in the process of fermentation. That's where we were. Then we looked up *wine,* but it didn't tell how to make it, really, and the library was closed. We were on our own.

About the bottles. We ran into difficulties because no one outside our group was willing to empty cola bottles; they weren't motivated. It was ten o'clock by then. Mac, Bill, and Whuff decided to check the houses along our street, avoiding the neighbors who thought of us as polluters, and staying far from that child, The Screamer. They said they were on a Scout bottle collection; that is, Mac and Whuff did. Bill said he was working his way through college, after two householders thought he was a trifle old for a Scout; his moustache undid him.

Lying. I think that was where our trouble started. One cannot lie. It doesn't *work.* (Of course, I was living a lie, being employed at Sears when Mac didn't know it. Oh, heavens—not that I would ever make it to heaven.)

Whuff argued being a Scout was fair and square, because (1) he had been one, and (2) we were all good scouts. Well, weren't we? He should have been an English major; he was so adept at bastardizing language and meanings. He brought in the largest number of empty bottles, too, although he was taken aback when Sue said that someplace in the Bible it mentioned new wine shouldn't go into old bottles. Sue confounded us frequently.

Bill said then we would sterilize the bottles. He took charge and was plenty grim; either a bottle was sterile or it wasn't—there were no halfway measures. He made us do two batches over. By this time we were all padding around barefooted, and there was some discussion as to whether we should tread the juice out, but no one cared for the idea. Fungus, said Bill.

It was amazing, though. The bottles began to look terrific, all lined up on the counter, shelves, and in cartons on the floor. I mean, we were true vineyard workers. We made a ceremony out of my adding to each bottle a little must—one or two crushed grapes. They sank to the bottom, as was proper.

Caps. How would we cap the bottles?

Well, said Whuff, his cousin had a sort of lever thing, and when he got back from his trip he'd borrow it, and some caps.

"Corks are better," said Bill.

Whuffor glared. "It's gonna be caps because that's what we can *get*. You seen any corks lately?"

Bill admitted he hadn't. Actually, we were all so bone-weary, we couldn't argue, though I tried. "We can't leave the bottles open," I said weakly.

"Why not?"—Mac.

"The juice will turn to vinegar, I *think*. Or . . . maybe it's bugs Mother worried about."

"The stuff has to *work*," said Bill. "It must have oxygen."

"Nuts." Mary's voice was thick with fatigue. "You're thinking of the patient you had yesterday, or was it last week?"

Sue said, "Somewhere I read yeast is involved. I have three yeast cakes; my aunt gave them to me. It only takes a tiny, tiny bit to make the juice work. Of course, the cakes are a little old."

"Old yeast is okay," Mac pointed out. "Better. It should age."

"Maybe this will turn out to be beer," said Whuff. "We ought to consult the Beer Baron and *Frau*."

Mary stared at him. "Whoever heard of grape beer?"

"For beer you have to have hops," said Bill.

It was my turn to stare. "You mean, you jiggle it?"

"Oh, God," said Mac. "No, Katie. Hops are—uh—they grow in the fields."

"However would I know?" I felt snotty, and I was snotty. "It takes a lot of *ignorance* to do what we're doing."

"Boy, will I sell vegetables tomorrow," said Whuffor. "Hops."

We looked up beer. Yep, you used yeast. We told Sue to go upstairs and get her cakes; we'd experiment. Sue left, and she didn't come back. We waited and waited. Whuff went after her. He didn't come back, either. The rest of us decided we ought to check. I was the last out of the kitchen. Going up the stairs I could barely move, and with each step it was more difficult.

Mr. Swensen had varnished the hallway and steps.

I could hear Mac, Mary, Bill, Whuff, and Sue on the landing, sort of slupping. I retreated, step by sticky step, and sat down in our doorway, then scrooched across the floor, feet up from the rugs (a hard way to get around, but I made it), and reached the cupboard in the kitchen where the dear old turpentine was. If our lives continued like this we'd be the world's largest users of turps. I got out some old rags and wiped off my feet and was washing them in the sink when I heard Mac at the door. Ran to him, handed over the can. He disappeared; soft sucking sounds, upwards. It was some time before he came back, and he sat on the rug, the way I had, feet in the hall. I took him a pan of water and a rag, and he handed me three cakes of yeast. He then used the turpentine, washed, and went to bed. His muttering had a dire sound; I guess he had nothing left but swear words.

Bitterly, I crumbled the yeast, thinking how rotten everyone was to conk out on me, dropped a tiny particle in each bottle as per instructions, and followed Mac to bed. It was 4:30 A.M.

As we were drowsing off (actually, it was as if we had been hit by two bricks), we heard Whuffor's truck roar outside. I didn't have enough energy to worry about him, but did have a fleeting hope his foot would not stick to the gas pedal.

Breakfast the next morning was chewing and swallowing, looking at the bottles, and smelling the juice doing whatever it was doing. Mac went to work, and later I took off for Sears.

Mr. Swensen never said a word about the varnish. Neither did we. However, we all read the sign he posted on the outside door when we dragged home from work. NOTICE: THE HALL AND STAIRS WILL BE SANDED AND VARNISHED TONIGHT. KEEP OFF!

We were happy to comply. About nine, Sue phoned and

asked us never to mention the day just past to her husband; he had called her from Echo Lake, and that was in the opposite direction from where he was supposed to go. Sue gathered he had done all right, in a business way. He simply didn't want it mentioned.

My feeling was the same. I hated to have customers looking at my lavender hands, and one old lady asked, "What ever is the matter, dear?"

I said, "Heart condition. It will pass now that I have the proper medication."

She was so sorry for me she bought a sheer black nightgown for the daughter-in-law she didn't like. I guess she was grateful I was not a member of her family.

At noon I bought some bleach and scrubbed up. The aura of eau de chlorine seemed to alarm people even more than purple palms. Customers are very touchy and must be handled with care; they are fragile.

When Whuffor returned home he brought the lever thing for caps, plus the caps, and the clan sealed the bottles. We carried them down the basement and put them on the dusty shelves Mr. Swensen indicated.

"I yust don't know," he shook his head, "if you know fut is fut."

He was correct; we didn't know what was what. But we were optimistic. And, as Mac said, I had discovered a group was not all bad, and that total effort could accomplish a good deal.

On Friday, the girls at the hospital in Ward AB loved the wine story. Slem laughed her head off; she said it would probably blow up. Angie slapped her, and it looked like trouble until Slem apologized. I don't think she had ever said she was sorry in her whole life before that. The attending psychiatrist looked at me strangely when I told him about the incident. "You're doing an extraordinary job," he said.

Ah, Eric—this isn't what I'd planned to do for you. Oh, my brother. "But I'm not really any good, you know. Doctor, they told me all the mistakes we made about the wine, and I was about to yell for help. Also, my sewing has *not* improved."

"See that it doesn't," he said, and laughed.

I thought he was almost as peculiar as the patients, but then psychiatrists probably are; in order to understand the quirks.

5

It seemed almost everything had gone wrong on my job that *could* go wrong. In one way, I was making progress. I understood Mac's problems better; I knew, more or less, what his days were like—the aggravations, the successes and failures, the *trying*.

The difference was, and this was vital, Penneys was *us*. Our future. I was loyal to Sears, and it would break my heart to be fired or to make a serious mistake that would hurt the store. Still, if I was fired, all would not be lost; there was Mac and Penneys. (Would Mr. Clift repossess the pots and pans? Would he garnishee Mac's salary, which might make the J. C. Penney Company unhappy? Oh, I mustn't lose the job.)

I was also beginning to comprehend the fascination of the retail business. I liked it, even though I was not good on the tax and stuff, and had trouble adding. The cash register was smarter than I was, for sure; though vicious.

The day I met the wife of the Great Mogul, recently retired head of the store, will go into my autobiography, which I shall write in thirty years, providing I live that long. At the rate I'm going, tension will cut me down early. I have read anxiety kills more people than anything else, and I have been anxious since birth.

I was waiting on two customers at once and feeling *fine* (a danger signal I never recognize), when a beautiful person came along. She had that patient look, and was tall, and her eyes were soul windows. Because of her personality, I decided I could handle *three* customers simultaneously; it's the action that's fun in retailing. Customer One was looking at bras, and I showed her a "no-seam" bra, but she didn't care about seams; she desired straps that were secure and that *lifted*. So I found some for her, rang up the sale, and wrapped them up. Skidded back to Customer Two, cracking my hip on the sharp corner of a display table. I ignored the pain, stifled a sob—the customer is the ultimate. Well, ole Number Two was returning three pairs of knee socks; too small for her daughter and how ever did that happen. I found the right size, wrong color, for her. She decided on a refund. So I asked Customer Three (beautiful) to wait for a minute, please, and reached for the refund book. It was not on the shelf under the cash register where it was supposed to be. Adrenaline started pumping through my blood vessels, arteries, what ever. I scrabbled around, smiling like the boy on the burning deck, or the one who said, "I'm killed, Sire," and fell dead.

I mean, if you lose a refund book, think what can happen. Someone picks it up, writes his own refunds around the store and leaves with enough funds for an easy life for a long time. Opportunity with a refund book is almost unlimited.

I knelt and examined the shelf. Nothing. Discovering nothing weakened my knees so much I had to hang on to the counter to stand up. I tried to think, but when you are desperate you can't do it very well; the mind scatters.

Customer One had left, satisfied. Customer Two was tapping her foot. Customer Three had brought two sweaters to the register, which was helpful, although one would expect it of her. I refrained from fainting and did a quick crawl around the cubicle, looking for the refund book on the lower shelves.

"What in the world are you doing down there?" asked Two.

"Hah. Hah," I said. "Trying to locate the refund book."

Said Three (beautiful), quietly, "Could it be in the drawer?"

With a tremendous surge of hope, I pulled open the drawer. It wasn't there. "I went on my break," I babbled, "and the girl in the next department took over because my relief wasn't in yet. The refund book has disappeared, and if I do not shoot myself, Mr. York will surely save me the trouble."

Trembling, I called security; in the vulgar vernacular, the house dicks.

Customer Two tapped her foot some more and announced loudly she did not have all day. She wanted her refund immediately because she didn't come into town very often and had a doctor's appointment. I needed one myself right then.

I said, "One moment, please." (Telephone operator; page 7, paragraph 6.)

Security came in the person of a pompous potbelly; I preferred him to the nervous skinny one who arrived a few minutes later. They asked different questions at the same time, and while I was attempting several answers, the girl in the next department took in the scene, came over, and said, "Katie, I borrowed your refund book."

"Next time you sign an IOU, or I will cut out your liver."
I don't know why I chose liver; stress and strain, I suppose.
I am not fond of liver.

I hugged the refund book; it was the U.S. Mint, my job,
my sanity. Crisis over, security melted away, as they always
do. I wrote the refund, straightened my halo, and took the
sweaters from Customer Three.

She handed me a discount card. It was blue.

I sagged. "I've never seen one of these."

"You don't know about the check list?"

"I don't know anything."

She explained and told me what to do, and I did it,
dropping my pencil three times in the process.

She helped me put the two sweaters into a bag (couldn't
get it open by myself). There were more customers. One
was beginning to fidget, and another was considering it.

I said, "Oh, that was a frightening experience."

Three agreed. "And you are still having a reaction. Now
remember it came out right, and forget it. You're doing
very well."

Although her mogul husband had retired, he had influ-
ence. He knew practically everyone in the chain, including
the chairman of the board—believe me, they wouldn't have
to go that high to get rid of Katie—and there were all the
men to whom the Mogul had given a start. Some were
grateful although, people being what they are, fewer than
you'd expect.

It doesn't pay to upset any customer, but it especially
doesn't pay to upset a mogul's wife, or an exec's wife,
retired or not. If I had known then what I know now (story
of my life), I'd have recognized the patient expression. The
wives of dedicated retailers have that look. They need it,
too. *Some,* of course, are meanies who accidentally married

a good man, usually not at the beginning because they don't have the stuff to stand by in the early days when things are rough. These wives demand extra service. I once rewrapped a doggy bag from a nearby restaurant because the exec's witch didn't want her friends to know she was taking home a doggy bag, contents for her own consumption. She must have had lousy friends, and I am sure she was the same.

Even if I had never found the refund book, I feel sure Customer Three would not have told her husband. She understood, and had a long memory. Perhaps she had worked at Sears when she was young; she was the type who one could tell had been young once, didn't mind getting older, and still liked young people. A very rare type.

Despite my traumas, I was gaining. It never comes easy.

That night at dinner I quizzed Mac. I asked him what was the most important job in the store.

"Mine," he said.

"Seriously."

"I am serious. Look, every job is important. Maintenance, stock clerks, manager, department manager . . ."

"You mean division manager?"

"No. We don't have division managers. Where'd you hear that? We have department managers."

He didn't give me a chance to answer, thank goodness.

He added, "One of these nights I'm going to ask Mr. Marcy to dinner. His wife is out of town."

"He'd probably prefer to eat at the country club," I said, hoping.

"No. He likes home cooking."

"When are you going to ask him?"

"Can't tell; it has to come sort of naturally, Katie. We don't want to be obvious, or make a production of it." He laughed. "There's a story—maybe it's true, maybe not—that a manager in the early days invited Mr. Penney to dinner, and the manager's wife borrowed a silver service and goblets, the works, from numerous buddies, and spent a week's salary on the food. When the meal was over, Mr. Penney asked, with deep concern, 'Are you sure you're living within your income?' That's a mistake we won't make—*borrowing*. Don't worry; Marcy is a good guy."

I wondered what Mr. Marcy would think of custard salmon loaf. Oh, steady on. I decided right then I'd wash the draperies and do the baseboards, and the following morning I did. I hung the hand-laundered draperies in the shower; they were heavy but would be dry in another twenty-four hours. After that, I polished the furniture and got to work on time. (I forgot to iron the newspaper, however; perhaps Mac would not notice.) I felt virtuous and efficient. The day went well, because I was at my peak. I shopped for groceries on the way home (decisions, decisions), and had just come in the door when the phone rang. Rushing to answer, I felt sure I'd won the surprise flight to Hawaii. I had entered the contest three weeks before and had a strong hunch I would win. Imagine. Thanksgiving in Hawaii! Free.

It was Mac on the phone. He said, "Hey! Put some more water in the soup!" That was a joke? "Mr. Marcy is coming to dinner, and Bill Phillips, buyer from the New York office, will be with us. Where've you been? I've tried to get you all afternoon."

"I was marketing." I had *not* bought soup.

"Good! See you in about an hour"—softly—"I love you, Katie."

"I love you, too," I said, like a parrot. At the moment, I did not. I went into the bathroom to wash my face, which usually makes me feel better. This time it didn't because there were the draperies hanging limply and wetly from the shower bar. In shock, I went back into the kitchen and examined the two very small pork chops. They had not grown while I was gone.

As I stood, paralyzed, the sack of groceries slowly, slowly fell over and a plastic bag of lima beans broke, spilling across the floor. They looked like pebbles on the beach. I seriously considered running away.

While I was considering, my nose told me that somewhere something good was cooking. I followed the nose to Sue and Whuffor's apartment. Sniffed. Rang the bell. It was Sue's day off; she had a kettle of corned beef simmering and was about to put in the cabbage, she said.

"Hold everything." I explained my situation and came forth with a proposition: if she would lend me the kettle and contents today, I'd give her my chops for their dinner tonight, and tomorrow I would cook corned beef and cabbage in the exact weight and proportion I was borrowing.

I don't suppose I was absolutely clear, but Sue was quick. It was a deal.

"Pray, Katie," Sue said. "If these jokers like corned beef, you're made. People either *do* or don't."

"Yar."

"You have lettuce? Tomatoes? Dressing?"

"Yar."

"Tossed salad, then."

We heard Mary coming up the stairs and met her, with kettle. We were explaining when I said, "Oh, God. The draperies! I washed them."

Mary got it. "Our color scheme is similar to yours; windows measure the same. I'll bring mine down on the rods— we'll put them up. Hey . . . what's for dessert?"

I hadn't thought that far.

"Mrs. Swensen has two apple pies cooling on the sill," said Sue.

We banged on Mrs. Swensen's door as we went by. She came across the hall. Sue told her. Mrs. Swensen went back and returned with a pie. "Mister'll never know I made two," she said.

"Is he painting anything tonight?"

"Pinochle at Olaf's right after supper," she said.

We were safe, then.

Sue backed out of the bathroom on her hands and knees; she was scrubbing the floor. "Some men have a thing about clean bathrooms," she said.

"Centerpiece," shouted Mary.

We all jumped.

"No flowers." I was firm. "They'll think I'm putting on."

"True." Mary thought. "Have to be careful about that. Oh, men! They naturally expect great food on short notice, but if you gave them something fancy, they'd figure you were extravagant."

"There certainly is nothing fancy about corned beef and cabbage," I said.

"Jiggs likes it," Mrs. Swensen nodded.

"Jiggs?"

"Comics; comical. Maggie thinks corned beef is low class."

"It's the way it smells," I said. "Once you pass the olfactory test, you're hooked forever."

"Centerpiece," said one-track Mary. She opened a cupboard door, grabbed a small red mixing bowl from its nest, and went outside.

Sue was now straightening the pictures on the wall. I set the table, stainless steel. One of Mrs. Swensen's first bits of advice to the bride (me) was to be sure the table was properly arranged when Mac came home. Then, even if I didn't have dinner ready, he'd *think* it was coming soon. A tired wage earner, said Mrs. Swensen, ought to know food was on the way.

I reflected gloomily, as I placed the napkins, that Mary's draperies looked better than mine, which were now reposing in the *Shaws'* shower.

Mrs. Swensen tasted the corned-beef juice. "Needs more salt." She added some.

Mary came back. She had picked some of the yew with red berries.

"Mister will murder you." Mrs. Swensen started to shake.

"He won't notice. These twigs are off the back of the bushes."

"Get dressed," Sue told me.

"I *am*." I had on my quiet purple with yellow stripes. If it was good enough for Sears, it was . . .

"You are *not*. Where's that navy-blue shift you wear with pearls?"

"No pearls. Went out with Whistler's Mother," I said. "Shift is a trifle short. I bought it for sub-teaching."

"Short. Well, all right. Whuff admires your knees. You have to be subdued. It's Mac's bag. Remember you're only background music."

"They can take me as I am."

Mary—"Bill says no one can stand anyone as they *are*. You are no exception, Katie Macfarlane."

True, I thought.

"I have a string of pearls. Cultured," said Mrs. Swensen, and she dashed out the door. I didn't know if she thought pearls were for cultured people, or if they were cultured pearls. Now was not the time to find out what she meant, however.

I went in the bedroom and put on my blue shift. Mrs. Swensen returned and put the pearls on me. I was pure B.A. major. Mary fastened my hair back. I felt like a department-store display-window mannequin.

"There they are," said Sue. "We made it."

A Lincoln was maneuvering up to the curb—a land-going yacht.

"I am going to be sick."

"You are not," said all three, and they scuttled out.

I watched the Continental, hoping it was the undertaker.

Mac got out of the back seat. Two large and handsome men emerged from the front; the three came down the sidewalk, up the steps.

I opened the door as they arrived. "Welcome!" I trilled.

Fact is, I liked our guests immediately. The New York buyer had on a colored shirt, and he was with it. He didn't have much hair, but his sideburns were magnificent. New Yorkers, I have noticed, and Hollywood types, have a tendency to compensate.

Mr. Marcy had more hair on his head and shorter sideburns, bearing out my theory. He sniffed and asked, reverently, "Is that corned beef cooking?"

"I'm afraid so," I said, very much the bride. "I suppose you'd prefer something else, but this is what we were going to have."

"I'm in luck." He was delighted. "My wife hates it, but I—ah!"

"Smells like my favorite pub," said Bill Phillips, the New Yorker.

Pub. I was going to explain we were often *aware* in the hinterlands, too, but refrained because it wouldn't be courteous, and also because of Mac's puzzled expression. He was examining the draperies, and knew the kettle wasn't ours, and was observing the table, centerpiece, *et al.*

It took him about ten minutes to recover. Fortunately, the business of taking off coats, hanging them in the closet, and the usual discussion of the weather (wonderful autumn day) spared us awkward silence.

I put on the coffeepot, added the cabbage to the simmering kettle, and started chopping the salad. I can do salad in my sleep, and take pride in shaking the dressing in true chef fashion (it's a mix, but in my own jar, so they didn't know), adding herbs and pepper, then tossing.

"Nice place," said Mr. Marcy, looking at the chair I hadn't seen Sue bring from their apartment. "Cozy."

"We were lucky to find it."

"In New York you'd pay a fortune for this," said Bill Phillips.

"So I understand. Not here, though. And we have wonderful, wonderful neighbors."

Mac grinned suddenly.

The men were all in the kitchen by then, fascinated by my salad toss, which is abandoned. I can let myself go.

We had a good time. The cabbage was right—firm, not soft; the corned beef tender. Salad excellent. I had never enjoyed a dinner more. There is nothing better than a meal someone else has cooked with loving care.

The pie was unbelievable. The crust was flaky and perfectly browned—apples and crust tasted as if they had been kissed by the sun. Mr. Phillips was on a diet (another thing that New Yorkers usually are), but he accepted, groaningly, a small second piece. He said he couldn't help himself and would starve tomorrow. Mac was so confounded when I brought on the dessert, clearly homemade, his mouth fell open, foolishly.

After the pie, the men talked business while I cleared the table and poured more coffee. Mr. Marcy mentioned ringing up sales.

"Did you ever have a cash register drawer come out and hit you in the stomach?" I was carried away by success.

Mac looked startled, but Mr. Marcy started laughing; he began telling us about when he first went to work at Penneys. It was fascinating, and he was witty about some of the things that had almost overcome *me*. I decided right then I would try to look on the bright side when at work.

I was so enthusiastic I said, "Would you like a liqueur?" Mac nearly fell off his chair.

"Well . . ." said Mr. Marcy. "What do you have?"

"*We* don't have any," I explained, "but the young doctor upstairs is always being given something by pleased patients, and his wife says they don't want it, really."

"You *do* have good neighbors," said Bill Phillips.

"We are careful about paying back," I added, hastily.

Mac took another look at the draperies.

The men agreed a B & B would be just right. Now, my family didn't drink liqueurs, and not much of anything else. I didn't know what a B & B *was*, but excused myself and went up to Mary and Bill's. Explained my mission. Then the Campagnas' door opened, and they came over. We all talked in hoarse whispers.

Whuffor said a B & B was Cognac and Benedictine. (I would think they would call it a C & B.) Bill had a bottle of each, which we found after an intensive search. Whuffor went back to his apartment and brought some cordial (he said) glasses. He said a B & B, not ready mixed, was hard to fix. First he poured some Benedictine into the glass; then he poured Cognac across a table knife because the Cognac was supposed to float and not sink into the Benedictine. This was difficult, but a table knife slanted into the glass helped the Cognac remain on top, somehow. It took Whuff two or three tries on every glass. The unsuccessful attempts he and Bill drank at once, then started over.

Whuff finally got four glasses that were satisfactory. Mary put them on a little plastic tray (we rejected a silver wedding-gift tray), and with warnings ringing in my ears advising no jogging, I went slowly down the stairs. The warnings were funny because Whuff and Bill had become increasingly hearty and hilarious. When I left, they were mixing their own liqueurs in jelly glasses. Every good party, said Bill, ended up with jelly glasses.

Mr. Marcy and Mr. Phillips and Mac agreed our neighbors were worth knowing, indeed. A great B & B was a work of art . . . and these were great.

I desperately hoped someone would give us Benedictine and Cognac for Christmas, so I could pay back painlessly, but doubted it would happen. I tucked that concern back in my head, along with living a lie, and the pots and pans. (It was getting somewhat crowded in my head.)

The gentlemen left at ten, a respectable hour. We went out with them to the Lincoln, and introduced them to Randolph on the way. Randolph was growing his full winter coat, and he was absolutely unique. Mr. Phillips said he'd like a dog like that, but we explained Randolph was universally beloved and practically mutually owned. We hadn't met his owner yet, but were looking forward to it. Then Randolph did something enchanting. He sat down and offered a paw to each gentleman. He had never done it before, and rarely repeated it. Randolph had a sense of the fitness of things.

As the Continental drove off, purringly, I said. "Materialistic. I'd rather have a Ford."

"It is a Ford," said Mac. "The best. Materialistic it may be, but I intend to buy one someday. What's the matter with driving a big Ford, or do you think we ought to travel by ox cart?"

"Ox cart, certainly. Consider the ecology. If we ever have a big car, Mr. Stafford Macfarlane, you'll have to put a mask on the —uh—"

"Transmission," said Mac, and laughed.

I knew he was only trying to mix me up, and I patted Randolph and thanked him and kissed him on the ear. He trotted off for home, wherever that was.

When we closed the apartment door, Mac put his arms around me, held me close. "Oh, Katie, I was proud of you . . . what *were* we having for dinner, by the way?"

"Two small pork chops." We both laughed. "It was the meat special again, and payday isn't until Friday."

"Yeh, but what's for tomorrow?"

"Chops for us; Sue buys. Corned beef and cabbage for Sue and Whuff; we buy."

"On special?"

"No. We will have scrambled eggs the following night. High on protein; cheap."

"What was with the draperies?"

"Washed ours. They weren't dry."

"Better get rid of the yew bowl. Mister would have three hundred fits if he saw it."

"Make that an even thousand fits. Will dispose of yew."

"Katie, how you managed—that dinner. It meant a lot to me. A man wants to be proud, you know? And when I couldn't reach you earlier, and I had already committed us, well—I worried. I knew it wasn't right to bring them here without letting you know sooner. It just happened. All the way home I wondered if . . . uh . . . you had more than two chops."

"Mac, somehow, some way, I'll always try to come through for you." Behind my back, I held up three fingers for Sue, Mary, Mrs. Swensen.

"YARL! Hip, hip, two-three-four . . ."

Mac and I were puzzled. We stepped out into the hall. Whuff and Bill were leaning against each other on the landing. Then, precariously, they inched down the stairs, had a little difficulty with the doorknob, and managed to get outside. On the steps, they congratulated each other over the accomplishment.

"Kinda foggy," said Bill, speaking of the clear autumn night, "an' a walk'll clear it up."

The boys had a bun on.

"I'd better settle accounts with the girls in the morning," I told Mac. "There's an awful quiet in the top apartments."

"Where'd they get it?"

"Whuff was mixing the liqueurs, and the ones that weren't perfect, they drank. I suppose it was basically our fault."

Mac understood. "Very good men have gotten into trouble testing like that. Good thing they each have a co-pilot."

We did the dishes. I told Mac about the pie, too, as well as the pearls. Neither of us could settle down; we felt responsible for Bill and Whuff, and it was a great relief when we heard them return. The fresh air seemed to have helped a little, but their involved conversation before they got up enough courage to enter their separate abodes was a classic in both procrastination and rationalization.

"God, they are silly," said Mac.

"Yes. Have you ever thought how lucky we are that none of us is any sillier? I mean, B & B is nothing we're going to have much of—but suppose someone was involved with pot all day, or hard stuff?"

"You mean 'smack'?" Mac smiled.

"No. I mean heroin. You made your point on that some months ago." I shook my head. "I surely was *young*."

"That's the real problem. Kids . . ."

"Young and lucky." I was thinking back.

I poured out the dishwater; Mac hung the third damp dishtowel on the rack.

"How did you happen to ask Mr. Marcy about the cash register? It was a stroke of genius."

"Let me take my shower and I'll tell you," I said. The time was now, I thought. I had to explain about Sears.

I took a long shower and manicured my nails and put on my best nightie; Mac thought sheer was more exciting than nothing. When I finally went into the living room, the head of the household was asleep in the borrowed chair. He looked defenseless and dear and innocent, though I well knew he wasn't all of those things. Yet something about the little lines around his eyes, and lips—firm even in sleep—helped me to understand the evening had been as difficult for him as it had been for me. Even more so. Not that our guests were ogres, or men to be feared. They were good guys who'd been there. They knew how life was in the potato patch, and they were sympathetic—especially with corned beef and apple pie tucked under their belts. Nevertheless, it had been a strain; their opinions were important to us. We wanted to make a good impression, something our parents probably thought we didn't care about. We *did* care. Everyone cares, even the wild, doomed ones who run with their own kind—impressing their counterparts in the only way they can.

Our evening had been a success; we knew it. There would be more. The best part was I felt certain the first hurdle was the hardest.

I hated to wake Mac, but I did. "I have something to tell you, darling."

He blinked, stood up slowly. "In the morning," he mumbled and stumbled into the bedroom, more or less falling into bed. There was no point in mentioning that he hadn't brushed his teeth.

I sat on the stool I used at the built-in vanity and heard his steady sleep-breathing. I watched him, and I loved him. I forgot he liked his job and found it exciting, as I did mine. All I could think of was the tiredness etched on his face, the weary slump of his shoulders as he had gotten out of the chair a few minutes before. I was suddenly angry: at his long hours; that he (and I) could care what two men might think about our life style; over the hard physical work often required of him. (Merchandise doesn't come in little boxes such as are on the counters; it usually arrives in huge crates and must be unpacked.) I was angry at the paper work that took so much time, and at uncaring, inconsiderate customers who demanded the impossible as if it were their right. I gave infuriated consideration to aching arches and marbled veins in legs that turned to stone from standing around on a slow day. I recalled the sadistic cash registers, rattlesnakes with a warning ting and then *whammo!*

It was great working for Penneys, because most of the top men, store managers, and district managers remembered how tough it was. Tactful and considerate, truly knowledgeable, they helped by suggesting improvements and handed out "well done" comments whenever possible; they inspired devotion, both to the man and the job. But there was the executive, fortunately rare, who was power prone; he fancied himself in the guise of a prosecuting attorney. Sarcasm was his forte, and bullying tactics came easily. For example, a day or two after inventory, when stocks were low and not always in order, a session with such a type reduced exhausted underlings to near desperation.

There was no point in offering an excuse, even when it was reasonable; logic was useless. The victims of these dictators took it; they took it and faced up to it and never, never forgot or forgave. An occasional jacking-up, a talk about real goals, a hard appraisal—these were necessary, at times, and even appreciated. It was the diminution of the individual that was both unforgettable and dangerous to morale.

Sitting there, I devoutly hoped the Small Caesars we knew would meet with deserved disaster.

Then I managed to work up a fury toward people who lived as they pleased, taking everything—psyching out, tuning out, and expecting men like Mac to pay the freight.

This was getting me nowhere, so I went to bed; couldn't sleep, which was just as well because I would have awakened fast enough half-an-hour later when Bill and Whuff started singing upstairs.

They were harmonizing: *The Dutch Company Is the Best Company*, etc. Their own foul version.

"We will never have any B & B again," I said.

Mac sat up. Listened. The tempo increased.

"Dear heaven," I moaned, "my father's outfit used that for a theme song, World War II."

Mac relaxed. "'All things are the same,'" he murmured. "'All things now are as they were in the day of those whom we have buried.'"

Mac! "Where'd you get that?"

"Marcus Aurelius; born 121 A.D. Alphonse Karr sort of paraphrased it 'bout 1849. '*Plus ça change, plus c'est la même chose.*'"

My smattering of French had departed. "Meaning?"

"Loosely—'The more things change, the more they are the same.'"

He impressed me vastly; he was so damned smart.

Neither of us went to sleep.

I forgot Sears.

And everything else.

I've read Marcus Aurelius; he'd understand. And so would Alphonse Karr, I'm sure.

I hoped, as I drifted off, Mac would understand, too. About Sears.

6

Although I chewed and swallowed along with Mac at breakfast, that wasn't actually my nature. I'm really a morning person—one of the ways I differ from most English majors, who are night people. Mac was unlike the average B.A. because he preferred the evening hours. After we were married, it took him a week to tell me, unhappily, he despised light and/or loud laughter, intelligent conversation, and questions such as: "What's your favorite color?" during the early A.M. As time passed, my first thought upon waking —and I had a strong urge to articulate it—was the state of the budget. But it came to me that Mac had to concentrate for an hour or so on functioning; it was vital for him to start the day quietly. So I kept still. If I was thrilled by dawn dewdrops sparkling in the grass, I enjoyed them by myself, even though it would have been twice the pleasure to share the beauty. A bird soaring, a shaft of sunlight— these had to be my private domain before breakfast. In turn, Mac kept the TV and transistor on low volume after 10:00 P.M. Our compromise worked out well in the apartment; the Swensens appreciated us.

I appreciated the entire apartment population.

The morning after we entertained the business guests, I knew better than to mention Sears, but I did venture a small suggestion. "Mac, let's have the group for Thanksgiving dinner."

He chewed the cereal reflectively.

"How about it?"

"Ever cook a turkey?"

"No."

Mac chewed the milk. (He always chews milk.)

"A turkey resembles a chicken," I said.

"Bigger, much. Hard to handle." He stirred the coffee. "We haven't had a whole chicken yet. Only legs."

"Turkey is inexpensive. There are leftovers."

"Do it," said Mac. "Do it, but let's not talk about it now."

I had thought Whuffor would be obligated to a relative or two or three or ten, but Sue confided we were helping them. Since they would be with us, either no relative would be offended, or they all would. She couldn't decide which was better.

Mary explained Bill was on call on Thanksgiving Day, but we could leave the doors open and hear the phone. We both knew we could always hear their phone, but would make the gesture for the Swensens, who had long ago decided the apartments were soundproof; if there was any noise, it was the fault of the tenants.

When I invited the Swensens, Mister said, "Yah, Sharlie!"

Mrs. Swensen sighed. "Poor Olaf. He will be all alone." Olaf was from their home town in Norway, and I said we would be pleased if he came, too.

When I told Mac about the extra guest, he moaned. "A Scandinavian invasion."

I laughed.

"Those Vikings are tough people, as the Scots know," said

Mac. "We had a lot of trouble with them a long time ago."

"Like 1066?"

"Like earlier, and the Normans in 1066 were Norsemen. Later, too. I am fairly sure there is old Norse in me."

I silently agreed, if he meant the stubborn part, which I occasionally referred to (not out loud) as bullheaded.

"We ought to ask Randolph," he added. "Give the party a French touch."

"Good idea." I would buy a bone for Randolph.

There are three basic steps to an invitation, as far as I am concerned. (1) You have to work up courage and tell yourself the dinner you are giving is weeks away, and you'll do everything ahead of time; then, if after such terrible contemplation you are still able to act, you proceed with the invitations. (2) The second phase is fun. The to-be guests' eyes sparkle—a party! Men think of food, women plan what they'll wear (and no dinner to get that night), and it is all wonderful. (3) Now comes the time for the hostess to hope no one will have a virus or other difficulty, and she considers the cleaning, shopping, and cooking. This is the most miserable period.

The *fact* of the dinner, the Moment of Truth, is frantic; I'm skittish right down to the wire. I have heard of people who love their own parties. If they are truthful, they surely have help with cleaning and cooking; perhaps even a butler to open the door. Usually I am stirring the gravy when the doorbell rings, and it lumps; the gravy, I mean. The whole occasion is absolutely *fraught*.

I much prefer to go to a party somewhere else than my own place. I can greet the hostess happily and stay as late as possible. At our house by party time, I'm so exhausted that if anyone remains after eleven, I start asking the Lord to get them out (*Oh, God, will they never leave?*).

For the three entire days immediately before my dinners,

I hate our friends. I have nightmares about the food, and imagine every kind of catastrophe—such as accidentally inviting killin' cousins to the same affair, which I once did. I hadn't realized they even knew each other, and naturally they had never brought up the subject.

One good point about that Thanksgiving dinner: everyone accepted at once, without waiting for a better invitation or saying they would let me know, and then *not*.

The reason I feel the way I do, explains Bill Shaw, looking very doctorish, is that I am insecure. He's absolutely right. How can you feel secure when you do not know how things will turn out? Our oven door slips, so I once dropped a roast on the floor when I meant to put it on the open oven (flapping) door. With a turkey, this would be a hanging offense. There is also the horrendous chance of presenting Thanksgiving-turkey guests with salmonella poisoning—an acute inflammation of the intestines associated with the bacteria. Even *my* imagination falters at the thought of sitting around the living room with sufferers from salmonella. As a matter of fact, they would all be either hospitalized or—light case—bedridden briefly.

One cannot talk about any of these worries because it is enough for the hostess to have a nerve crisis, let alone the people who come to break bread. (Not a bad idea; serving only bread would be fine with me.)

I was committed, as Mac pointed out, for Thanksgiving dinner.

I made paper turkeys and painted them, and cut out some rather pale Puritan lads and lassies from a magazine, pasting them on cardboard. The apartment could be decorated quickly. I'd wait until the last minute to buy mums (bunch price lowered to fifty-nine cents), but I had to choose the turkey in advance. The butcher put "Macfarlane" on the bird before he placed it in the deep freeze; I had a sort of premonition about my identity tag being there, in the turkey morgue. The one I had bought was not a name brand, but it was cheap. Anyway, the most important part was in the herb seasoning of the stuffing, and in the cooking.

Meanwhile, the festival of Thanksgiving was being celebrated at State Hospital. Instead of bedpan covers, we worked on Early American costumes for a skit the patients were going to present before the big meal.

Slem tried on a costume, and although it was somewhat small, she looked like the buxom wife of an English expatriate (Colonist) yeoman. Angie said all Slem needed was the honor seat on the ducking stool.

Slem didn't lose her temper. "Don't strain," she said. "I'd of had it made in Salem."

Barbara shuddered. "Witches."

"Thanksgiving is different, Barbara," said Angie, swinging on the old emotional trapeze. "We give thanks."

"For this?"—Alice.

"For what?"—Jeanie. One was Jean, now, and the other was "Jeanie with the light brown hair."

"*Thanks* that we are not chained in Bedlam," said Angie. "There's hope."

"Hope? Here?"—Lucy.

" 'A hope beyond the shadow of a dream.' Keats wrote it; I didn't."—Angie.

"All our hopes are shadows," Alice sang, in time with the ticking of her built-in metronome. Outside, she had been a concert artist, on the threshold of fame. I knew she would step through that doorway, someday. Someday.

"Damn it," Slem shouted. "Our hopes are real."

"I will not make an Indian headdress with chicken feathers," said Angie.

Unprintable, said Slem.

We did, anyway. At least we tried. As usual, mine was the worst; the chieftain's feathers scraggled. I put the headdress on.

Jean started laughing. "You look like a ruffled grouse."

Everyone laughed.

"All right, all right. So call me 'Grouse.' Let's get whackin'!"

Dr. Kintosky said, later, I was a natural.

"Grouse?"

Then *he* laughed. "No. Natural *natural*."

I looked at him. "You're borderline."

"Aren't we all?" he smiled, and meant it.

Penneys and Sears were more Christmas-oriented than Thanksgiving-minded. Mac was enthusiastic about a turkey made out of neckties at Penneys. Clever, he said. I was excited over the Sears musket display in sportswear, although I somehow refrained from telling him so.

On the Friday before Thanksgiving when I arrived at the locked ward, there was an air of excitement. Slem was going *out*. It was thrilling; she was ready. Angie was better, and Edith spoke occasionally. But Barbara . . . Barbara (I admitted only to myself she was my favorite) had been sent to another ward for further treatment. I closed my eyes and sent good thoughts to Barbara—lost, haunted, alone.

"She'll make it back," said Slem. "I swung like a pendulum a year ago."

I wanted to believe Slem.

I don't suppose holidays are pleasant for the patients in any hospital, but in a mental hospital a holiday is almost unbearable . . . not only for the patients, but for the personnel who work there, and care. At State, most of us cared deeply, and when someone went out of reach, out-of-sight-mind, we grieved. Sometimes, the very fact that it *was* a loved holiday set a patient back. Hardest of all was the paucity of visitors.

We finished the projects we'd been given in Ward AB. When the charge nurse came to let me out, she carried a large brown paper sack and presented it to me. The members clapped, as if it were some kind of a special prize. I had to promise not to open it until I got home. A present, they said, from friends.

I kept my word, of course—a good thing because when I delved into the sack, I was so touched I couldn't do anything at all for a while. Carefully wrapped in tissue paper was a Puritan family of four, exquisitely made. Those stitches by Angie—for her baby, Lawrence? No, for me. Progress. I had to look on the bright side. The painted doll faces were marvelous. (Barbara, I think.) I recognized the replica of me, and Father and Mother were almost right—it was their loving expressions that made them so.

Eric was . . . Eric. I had shown the members his picture, and someone had total recall. The figure had a tiny bundle against its shoulder, held tightly, and when I examined the bundle, I saw it was a papoose.

I sat there, numb. Then I unwrapped three Indians, and a miniature roast goose and turkey. I whispered, "Thank you . . . thank you . . . thank you."

After Friday, I was so busy with worrying about Thanksgiving dinner that I couldn't think much about Ward AB. That was as it should be; when one identifies constantly with the patients, the beneficial effect of coming from "outside" is reduced. That is what Dr. Kintosky had told me, and I believed him.

I had thought of asking for Wednesday before Thanksgiving off, but reconsidered. Either I was a crybaby, or I wasn't. I had the job, so I must get on with it. But that Wednesday at the store was spooked. First thing, a customer came in—she must have been waiting for the doors to open—with a tub top that I positively knew had been marked down twice. She said it had faded and demanded the original price. She had no sales slip. I tried to reason with her, but she was in no mood to make sense, especially with a kid type (her words) like me.

I rang Mr. York's bell.

She gave him a bad time, and when she left (sans refund), she said she would never shop at Sears again. She blasted me, the store, the manufacturer, Mr. York, the manager, and the words she used must have come from the same kind of cradleless home Slem was raised in, only worse. Mr. York had developed tough fibers, but I had not. I agonized over every incident. When a day begins like that, you can almost be sure it will continue in the same fashion. It did.

The Wednesday before Thanksgiving is not one of the biggest for shoplifters, but we had our share. I had found out from the other girls when I started working that I was lucky to have Fridays and Saturdays off because stealing increases then. We learn by exchanging information on our coffee breaks. I suppose the thief wants something free for the weekend; I always hoped it would be a jail sentence; I really did. Mr. York was more bitter about internal theft. He hated people who worked for a company and took advantage of their position to steal; he said they were betrayers. I was beginning to feel like Mrs. Sutler, the Penney detective; I didn't like any of the jerks.

For juveniles, shoplifting before Mother's Day and Father's Day was their notion of fun and games. That might seem touching to the bleeding hearts who have no interest in the retail business, but not to me. Even so, believing the way I did, I was sorry for the kids who stole. I guess they never thought of the gift they were sneaking for their parents—if caught (and they are, sooner or later). It's a session at the police station or in court. There is no joy in either place, and the kicks aren't worth the penalty. Never. Besides, as I have said, that bell tolls for *me*, and I don't have one cent to pay for tribute.

My tribute I pay to Mr. Clift, super-salesman.

After the hairiest day I ever spent, I went home and dug into our flour-bin savings. The doorbell rang.

It was Mr. Clift.

"I couldn't come on Saturday this week," he told me. (Friday was Mac's payday, and Mr. Clift wisely arrived the next day.) "So here I am."

He surely was.

I dusted my hands. "Mr. Clift, I do not have five dollars for you now."

"You don't have five dollars?"

"I *have*, but it's part of my turkey money."

"Oh."

"You look like the President."

"I do?"

"Yes. President Calvin Coolidge."

Mr. Clift beamed. "I have been told that before. I think it's the reason I sell a great many pots; I don't *look* like a salesman."

"No, you don't," I put my heart into it; he surely did not appear lethal. His process was painless, at the time. "President Coolidge was my grandfather's favorite."

"A trifle austere, and silent, which I am not."

He was so right.

But he looked dear, sort of; pleased and honored and trying to resemble even more The Hon. Mr. Coolidge. He reached in his pocket, pulled out an enormous roll of bills, and peeled off five dollars. He handed it to me.

"Why, I can't accept this." I gave the money back.

He bowed, his usually severe face wreathed in smiles. "Thank you, Mrs. Macfarlane. I shall mark your weekly bill 'Paid.'"

"But . . ."

"I have so much to be thankful for," he went on, earnestly, "I need to pass it on. My wife is home. Cooking for to-morrow. She hasn't been with me for two years."

"Where was she?" I always have to know how it turned out, or what happened.

"State Hospital. Now, with medication and out-patient treatment, she will cope."

"Cope?" I sounded stupid, I knew. I could not . . . I could *not* ask if his wife's name was Slem. It was unlikely, anyway—with the way she spoke, and his precise English. It was impossible. Or was it?

"Yes, and with this job I can always run by the house to see if everything is all right with her."

He loved her.

"But . . ."

He held up his hand, as if he were directing traffic. There was a lot of ham in Mr. Clift; Mac says every good salesman has ham. "Thank you for the payment, Mrs. Mac-farlane. Happy Thanksgiving. Good-by."

"Happy Thanksgiving to you, too!" I had to call out, he left so fast.

Was it Slem?

Thoughtfully, I walked to the market; borrowed a cart and pushed the turkey to the apartment, all uphill. Panting, I returned the cart to the butcher; he was so delighted to see it safe and sound, he gave me a beef bone for Randolph.

"People take the carts all the time," he said. "They seem to think they come with the meat and potatoes."

I sighed. *People.*

I bought mums for the table for sixty-nine cents; they weren't reduced all the way yet; I couldn't wait.

When I told Mac about Mr. Clift, he thought it was amusing—I mean, the switch of *me* selling the hot salesman.

"I didn't try to sell him anything at all!" I was indignant. "I told him the truth, and I never expected five dollars. I thought he would come back on Saturday."

Mac chuckled. "Katie, you are a very, very funny girl."

In the evening Mac went to borrow chairs for the guests (*from* the guests), but everyone said they'd bring their own next day; a sensible way to manage. They offered to bring plates, etc., but I had enough. It was late when we went to bed, about one o'clock. At two, Mac sat bolt upright.

"My God! Oh, God." He was *praying*.

I was terrified. "My God WHAT?"

"My God, I forgot to lock the back door. On the nights I work, it's my responsibility. Oh, God!" He had jumped out of bed and was wildly putting on his clothes.

I sat up. "I locked the door, Mac."

"Oh, my God, the door of the *store*—the J. C. Penney Company!" shouted Mac, and in a minute I heard the M.G. roar into life and jet takeoff.

I fell back and slept on the surface—coming to from time to time, and drifting off. Mac returned at three-thirty. He reported all was safe and sound—he was still sweating—and drank a glass of milk.

At five I got up, scrubbed the defrosted turkey, and put

the dressing I had made the night before in the cavities (as the cookbook said). I found two and thought there wouldn't be more, but I did have a psychic shock when I ran across the neck curled up in the breast cavity. Oh, dear heaven, that poor turkey. I had quite a time getting the neck *out*, along with the giblets, which I decided to forget about. I had enough on my mind. Perhaps Randolph would like them. I'd ask his owner, if I ever met the owner, and meanwhile the giblets could repose in the freezer part of our refrigerator.

I used Mother's turkey method. I had bought a piece of fine white cloth at the remnant counter at Sears, and I buttered it and tucked it snugly around the big bird, which weighed twenty pounds. We would have leftovers for a month, I thought, and I loved them—both as cook and gourmet. (Gourmet leftovers?) Of course, I was reckoning without Whuff, whose appetite was bigger than he was.

Turkey in the oven, I went back to bed. Hadn't been there long when Mac jumped and shouted, "Look at the time!" and started to dress.

"What's the matter?" I asked. I really was nervous, and silly, too. "How now, Brown Cow?"

"Going to work. We're *late!*" he was in a frenzy.

"It is Thanksgiving, Mac"—gently.

"Uh . . ." It came back—the experience with unlocked door. He sat on the foot of the bed. "Never, never again will that happen, Katie. I don't know *how* I forgot. Oh, God . . . thank God . . . no one realized . . . no one knew. Place was wide open."

He took a deep breath, and dived into bed, a sock dangling, and still in his shorts. He was asleep almost at once.

I understood; his day had been like mine; worse, probably.

The alarm went off four hours later. We could smell the turkey. Our first Thanksgiving! It was great. The cranberry sauce and mince pies were made; we were ready. We were so excited we forgot to be tired. Mac was not one to brood, so we barely mentioned his trip to College Plaza and the J. C. Penney store. But he would not forget it, I knew. Never.

We even conversed at breakfast. We were suave and civilized and put our plates on folding end tables and took them into the living room. We didn't want to disturb the beautifully set table, with the golden mums and yellow candles ready to be lighted. The little Pilgrim family, complete with papoose and Indians and fowl, was together under the flowers. It looked as if we'd had a bountiful harvest, and of course, that was what it was about—giving thanks for our blessings.

Time went quickly because there were the sweet potatoes to fix, and I made brown-sugar syrup to candy them. The celery wasn't properly curled so I set the refrigerator thermostat for lower temp. The radish roses were effective, the aspic salad a good color. All set.

Mac read the newspaper, which Mrs. Swensen had put under our doormat (already ironed, the dear), in leisurely fashion, like a king. After he finished he repaired a chair-leg and polished the TV screen, and went out to grease the M.G. as a reward for saving his career by charging off into the night. First, though, he opened the kitchen door a few inches so the smell of turkey roasting would permeate the apartment house. He looked sheepish when he did it, and I told him it was a good idea. Half the fun is anticipation.

When Mac came back from giving the M.G. its symbolic

carrot (grease), we dressed in our best. I wore my going-away suit; as Mother had pointed out, it would be right in any season. I owned one frilly apron, and put it on the counter, where it would be handy. Mac was handsome in the wedding suit he saved for VIPs when they visited Penneys. We were proud of each other.

It was nearly time for people to arrive. I remembered Mother removed the cloth cover from the turkey about now. Mac had to lift it out of the oven. I had managed to wrestle it *in* after stuffing, but then it was easier to handle. Mac put the disposable pan (we didn't have a roaster) on the bread board. He removed the cover.

The turkey was browned nicely, but it had *hair* on its chest. Each little hair stood straight *up*. I have never been more horrified in my life.

Mac said, "I guess we should have singed it."

"Singe?"

"Scorch. Gets rid of—uh—"

We had no time for argument, but I felt I had done enough for the bird, which I was worn out with and hated intensely for this final offense.

We could hear the Campagnas and Shaws talking in the upstairs hall. They were on their way.

Mac quickly locked the door. I ran to get the big scissors. Couldn't find them, and remembered they were with the sewing machine, in the closet, under the books. I grabbed my manicure scissors, rushed to the kitchen. Mac accepted the scissors and scrutinized the turkey with professional aplomb; he went over it with the flourishes of a born barber. How he could be so calm, I did not know.

There was thunderous knocking.

"In a minute!" I called, and nearly had a heart attack because they all had keys.

Unhurried, Mac finished the haircut, blew the residue

off onto a newspaper page I held, quaking. I was putting the folded paper into the garbage pail when he opened the door.

"Hi! Welcome!" Mac could change character in a flash; from barber to doorman was a cinch.

"A beauty!" breathed Whuff as he passed the turkey. I had never seen him eye a girl with such reverence.

Whuff put his and Sue's chairs in the living room, and Bill and Mary followed, with chairs.

"About ready," I said. "Turk has to brown a little more." Whuff helped Mac put the bird back in the oven; since the doors on the ovens in every apartment flapped, Whuff was aware of the danger.

We sat in the living room. I tried to visit but couldn't concentrate. Kept running into the kitchen to check various items. We waited for the Swensens. When the outside door to the apartment opened, we knew it was Olaf. In a few minutes, Mister and Mrs. and home-town guest were at our door. Olaf ("Call me Ole") was much larger than Whuff, who was momentarily upset because he wasn't accustomed to looking both *up at* and *around* anyone else.

Olaf bowed and presented me with a long, narrow, gurgling box. "Aquavit," he said.

"I beg your pardon?"

"Norske drink. You like potato?"

"Yes."

"You like caraway?"

"Yes."

"Yah," said Ole. "Vater of Liff."

"Liff?"

"For a long liff, and a happy one." He smiled. With the white-blonde hair, ice-blue eyes, even teeth—all to size— he resembled a radiant mountain.

"I hope so." I was nearly overcome.

He hit his chest. "Power. Vatch it."

"We are having sherry," I said.

"Yah." He turned to Mister and they spoke in rapid Norwegian. "Is too strong for now, but someday?"

"You're awfully kind. Thank you. We shall treasure the ... the ...."

"Aquavit." He pronounced it "akvavit." I had heard of the drink and I wanted no part of it; especially after our experience with the B & B. Potato and caraway sounded as if there were muscles in it. Certainly Ole had muscles.

He bowed again, and we shook hands briskly, which was good because one more bit of knuckle pressure and I would have been crippled forever; also my hand got lost in his.

Of course, one schedules the roasting of a turkey, but the butcher had told me to give this one a little longer. How long was that?

Mrs. Swensen said if you waggled a turkey leg, you could tell if it was truly ready. The difficulty with experienced cooks is they rely on a sixth sense that is missing in the inexperienced person; Mrs. Swensen's recipes had pinches of this and a smattering of something else. I often wondered how much a pinch was, exactly.

I went to the oven to check every minute or so, usually with an entourage consisting of Sue and Mary. Mrs. Swensen was the type of general who directed from behind the firing line. We three waggled a leg so much it came off, a terrible moment; clearly the turkey was done. I murmured it might be overdone, but Bill had acute hearing and he called in from the living room that poultry should always be well cooked because it could create certain health hazards.

It was well cooked.

We sat at the table. I asked Olaf to say the blessing. It was pleasant to hear it in Norwegian. His manner was serious and his deep voice deliberate. When he was through, the Swensens echoed, "Yah!" and we all fell to.

Ole and Whuff weren't competing—they were only being themselves. Halfway through the meal I gave up anticipating leftovers. At the rate they were going, we wouldn't have any. Whuff quit after the third helping, but Ole went back for the fourth. I don't believe Whuff would have stopped, but he had given an unexpected hiccup and Sue fixed him with a gimlet eye, so he refrained. Clearly, Olaf had saved himself for this day.

We viewed Ole with awe. I wondered how in the world the Northmen had carried sufficient food supplies in the boats they used for conquest. Probably they counted on plunder to keep them going. Later, out of curiosity I looked up Northmen, Vikings, Norsemen—they amounted to the same thing—and my theory was correct. Plunder they got, and they started around 800 A.D. Durable types—tough Teutons.

We saw another side of Mister. He and the Mrs. indulged in the same kind of flirtation they had at the art gallery. He was gallant; she giggled, and her cheeks grew more and more rosy. After dinner, I served coffee in the living room and passed the mints. It was a game with me; Whuff gave up on the fifth pass, but Ole accepted through the eleventh, when I ran out of mints.

The conversation was interesting; Ole had led a fascinating life. He'd been every place in the world, and his descriptions were original and perceptive. He'd sailed on early grain ships to China; he had been mugged in Hong Kong and Cairo and Marseille. (It must have taken ten men to do it.) He had been stabbed in Berlin and New

York, and shot at in various places. He had married four times in Tahiti. "Enough," he said. "Ay am a bachelor at present."

Bill listened, enthralled. I knew Olaf would be a case history. Bill viewed our guest with professional detachment, and kept asking questions. We all did. We couldn't stop. Ole tried his best not to occupy the center of the stage— he was far too courteous to monopolize the conversation —but there was no help for him until Mister spotted Randolph outside. We invited Randolf in for the beef bone. He sat up, accepted the bone with his lower teeth, gently and gracefully.

"Ay like the animal," Ole said. "Vill you sell?"

We laughed. I explained that charm was Randolph's stock in trade, and he didn't belong to us. Like Olaf, Randolph was a citizen of the world.

Mister grew restive, so the Swensens left with Ole. We knew they were aching to continue their pinochle tournament.

I shut the door into the dinette-kitchen; couldn't bear to have anything more to do with food, dishes, or the depleted turkey, which I had put into the refrigerator in order to avoid salmonella.

It was Mary's idea that we should start to play "stick match." She taught us how. You light a kitchen match, quickly blow it out and, from a sitting position (so the men wouldn't have advantage of height), throw it up against the ceiling. It sticks there, if properly tossed, which isn't often. The men were better at the game than the girls, but we caught on. I had been concerned about the plaster, but Mary pulled a match off the ceiling and it didn't leave a mark. We got to howling like maniacs. The game went on for a long, long time. When we were worn out with talk, laughter, and too much to eat, the Campagnas and Shaws left by the front door, taking their chairs. The way the apartments were arranged, there was a door from the back hallway into the kitchen, and a door from the living room into the front hallway. Everyone almost always used the kitchen doors because the garages were in back, as well as the bus stop. The keys unlocked all doors, of course.

After the guests had left, I was appalled by the forest of matches on our ceiling. Mac groaned, but got my vanity stool and took down the matches. I handed him a rag soaked with cleaning fluid and he also removed a few tiny charcoal dots on the ceiling.

"The game is all right with plaster," I said, "but wallpaper, no."

"So no wallpaper," Mac said.

So.

I sighed and wearily went into the bedroom to change into slacks and blouse, my cleaning-up costume.

"Do the dishes in the morning," Mac urged.

"Tomorrow is my day at State. Anyway, I can't get up and face the mess."

I opened the dinette door. Mrs. Swensen was caught in the act; she was drying the last, the very last, dish.

I hugged her. "Oh, you shouldn't! Oh, you've missed the pinochle."

She looked as grim as it was possible for her to look, which wasn't very. "Olaf brought aquavit to the Mister. They are both asleep. Ole on the davenport, Mister on the bed. Such doing." Then she began to laugh. "And you! All the time, I've been yust smiling until I hurt. You sillies!"

I told her the ceiling was undamaged.

"Only people get damaged," she said. "We do not worry about ceilings—don't tell Mister I said so. Ah . . . you are babies. . . ." Then she put her arms around me and rocked for a moment, as if I were the child she never had.

I thanked her some more. "During the prayer, I think you ought to know I counted you as a blessing."

That was enough for Mrs. She slipped out the door in a cloud of rosy blushes. I gazed at the immaculate kitchen. I knew in the morning I would be able to go to the hospital with composure and a clear conscience.

Thanksgiving time may be a triple holiday for some families, but not for those in the retail business. Fri. and Sat. after the turkey are terrific shopping times. Housewives have leftovers for dinner—they are free; the children are not in school and can go with mommy, or can be trundled along by daddy, who is off work. "Ooooh! There's Santa!"

Thanksgiving and Christmas are too close. Someone ought to give thought to that, although perhaps it's good. Harvest in, one must consider giving it away, which is what happens, basically, at Christmas, when there are gifts, cards, and decorations to contemplate. Some people might even have another turkey, if there weren't enough leftovers.

Mac left for work earlier than usual; he loved the Fri. after Thurs. Thanksgiving. I made the bed, gave the bathroom a fast scrub, and went to State. Observed sternly by the charge nurse—her expression indicated indigestion— I counted the needles and other dangerous objects, and was let into AB. With Slem gone "out," there was less vitality. I noticed it at once. As I unpacked the basket, feeling like Red Ridinghood visiting grandmother, I thanked my friends for the Pilgrim decorations.

I began to sense something seriously wrong.

"Aren't you glad to see me?" I asked. "I could hardly

146

wait to get here. We're making curtains for the visitors' lavs today. The material is pretty; they trust us."

"Visitors. Who has them?" Angie raised aristocratic eyebrows.

"We're glad you're here," said Lucy.

"We wanted you to come."—Jean.

"We depend on you."—Silent Edith.

Alice did not sing. She spoke carefully; there was no metronome ticking away, unseen, unheard by us. "Barbara ... Barbara ... killed ... herself."

I didn't ask how they knew. They always know. There's an underground in a hospital that would put foreign intrigue to shame. The patients usually know the difference between rumor and fact, too.

My knees gave way; I fell on the bench.

"Barbara bit her wrists and bled to death in the night," Angie said, crisply. "Too bad they didn't think to protect her from that."

I stared into space. Presently, I became aware of the members intently watching, as if my reaction were more important than anything else in the world.

I sat up straight. "Barbara had to go away," I said. "We needed her gifts, as we needed Eric, my brother. It would be good if they had not left, but we can remember them. As long as we do remember, they are here." I bowed my head and whispered, "'And if I die before I wake, I pray the Lord my soul to take.'"

It was all I could think of for Barbara.

I stood. "Barbara was no quitter, no matter how it seems. She was away when she did that. Next time I promise we'll work on our Christmas gifts, and if I can't swing it, there will be one big fracas around this place. Now, let's get whackin' at lav curtains."

We broke a record that day; we made more curtains

than any other ward, and made them better. We cut and stitched and perspired. When the charge nurse came in, she was amazed.

"You've accomplished so much!" she said. Her compliments were rare and we valued them.

"Barbara helped," said Jeanie.

7
🐾

Christmas.

We were strictly budgeted, and the only way to save for a house was to deposit the flour-bin money in the bank each month, leaving barely enough for expenses. I thought maybe I could make gifts.

Who, *me?* The seventh grade home-ec dropout?

About all I had to give was a happy smile and a hearty "Ho!Ho!Ho!" That was not enough, even for Mr. Clift.

I discussed the problem with my friends in Ward AB. We agreed any sewing I might accomplish would be an insult to the unfortunate recipients. Ward W in the hospital was painting candles, but I was no painter, and weight plus postage were expense factors. My lack of talent depressed us all.

Led by Angie, the ward members said if I would buy quality linen handkerchiefs, they would embroider the initials of Mac's and my relatives on them, providing staff permitted. When the charge nurse came we inquired, and she said, sniffing, sorry; NO. What if all volunteers expected patients to work on their private projects? Slave labor. Oh, *no.*

Angie blew. "What's your maiden name, Katie?" she hissed out of the corner of her mouth so the nurse couldn't hear.

"Rogers."

Angie then stated that most of her relatives' names started with "R." She said I would buy handkerchiefs for those relatives, and I would then mail the finished products to them for *her*. The red tape wound up on this one, and we weren't fooling the charge nurse for one minute, but it looked as if we had come up with an answer. Alice, Edith, and Lucy swore their relatives' names began with "M." The two Jeans drew straws and ended up with the children in our families (they'd do bunnies and baby chicks for them; in living color). By the time we finished with my list, there would be a beautiful, beautiful handkerchief for everyone.

Then, what could I give Ward AB? Jane had gone out soon after I came, followed by Slem . . . and Barbara. Six remained. My old gang. (We expected new members.) *What?*

We all argued over *that*, and at last agreed that everyone would do two handkerchiefs—one for her, one for me. I wasn't exactly happy with the solution, but it was a compromise—necessary, not satisfactory. There are few gifts that can go into the locked ward; even a comb can be dangerous for some patients. A mirror is unthinkable. Chewy candy is out, but small candy canes? The charge nurse said all right; we could *eat* them all at the next session. Ward AB would have other presents, of course; the Auxiliary was working on them—safe, soft, comforting.

Then I didn't know where to buy the handkerchiefs. Sears or Penneys? I had taken the girls into my confidence; they knew I was living a lie. They advised me to go to Penneys because it was Mac's bag, and many of the relatives were his. Good sense, I said.

"For you," sang Alice, "we have sense."

"For yourselves, too," I said. "Don't kid me, Alice. You've copped out for a while. Whatever, however, whenever—sometime you're going out and cope because you can. Okay?"

"How are the bears, Goldilocks?" They all knew I liked the old-old tales—Rapunzel and Red Ridinghood and Goldilocks.

"Flourishing. Let's get whackin'."

On Saturday I went to Penneys. Should have remembered discounts are not given on Saturday, which is the time for bona-fide customers. However, Mac let me make my choices. He would bring the handkerchiefs home, male and female (hankies have gender; men's noses are bigger, usually), on Tuesday when the discount was permitted. Tues. is not as busy as Sat., so employees can buy.

I delivered the goods to Ward AB the following Fri. The charge nurse smiled frostily, as was her wont. She'd had so many responsibilities that after twenty years her lips were frozen.

Then there were Mac's presents. Nothing could ever be fine enough for him. I wished I had a magic wand and could turn fifty peas into pearls. I would have had one pearl put into a tie tack, and sell the rest and buy him a yacht. Perhaps I might have pearlized a thousand peas. With a magic wand, anything is possible. I didn't have one, however.

At Sears I found, marked down, a heavenly sweater, Mac's size; cable knit. Masculine tan and green. It was perfect. I bought it.

———

After dinner that evening we went for a walk. If Mac had had the sweater he wouldn't have had to wear the suède car-coat, by now visibly used. I had tried to spot clean it; a serious error. Mac practically galloped. I had a hard time keeping up with him. When I complained, he slowed down, but presently would speed up again. He strode. I was almost running.

I said, "You're nervous, Mac."

"No."

"Yes."

"No."

"What is it?" A dreadful thought came to me; maybe Miss America or someone equally beautiful was working in his department. A girl like that could distract a man. Was Mac smitten? I stood still; he went on. I gathered energy and passed him in a spurt, stood in front of him.

"Tell me what the trouble is."

He looked at me. "Go back to the apartment, Katie. I'll be along. There's something I have to walk off."

I went home so downcast I didn't care if I ever saw another sunrise. It was an hour before he came in.

"Now?"

"Now." He sat down and told me. He had ordered a gross of iridescent beads, the kind that comes in little plastic containers. They are used to decorate all sorts of things, from dresses to dolls. A gross is twelve dozen. However, Mac had used a different kind of requisition form; he had been given another section to manage, a change from socks. The new form was preprinted in units of a dozen. What he had received was *one hundred and forty-four dozen* containers of beads, rather than twelve dozen.

"Yah, Sharlie!" I was stunned.

"I don't know how the order went through." Mac put his hands to his head, as if there were one big ache there. "No one caught it. It's my fault, and my department is going to be loaded with more beads than anyone would believe. It's so stupid, Katie; I didn't read the form. I mean . . . first I left the door open, and now this."

"Does Mr. Marcy know?"

"Not about the door, praise the Lord; and he will never know, but *I* do. That's soul-searing. About the iridescent beads he does know; the whole store is *shook*. Everyone, in fact, but Mr. Marcy. He didn't lose his cool. He said, 'No need to tell you, Macfarlane, after this, to check requisitions. Now, *get rid of those beads.*' "

"Did you ask him how?"

"I did *not* ask him how."

"Beads." I thought. Nothing came.

"Katie, what would you do with a million beads?"

"I'm not exactly handy . . . ."

"You have ideas, Katie." He was pathetic.

I closed my eys. "Make a collar for Randolph; cut out Christmas-tree shapes, smear glue and stick on beads. . . ."

"Hey!"

"Do the same with leather, either glueing or sewing, and come up with a headband à la Navaho. It's *in* to be Indian."

"Keep thinking."

"I'm finished."

"No, you aren't."

"Invent a dance—call it "Syncopated Sioux"; suggest iridescent-beaded shoe buckles or moccasins are necessary for the Synco; sell beads to teen-agers to sew on velvet chokers for mother's Christmas present. Make sand paintings, but with beads, not sand. Mac, I can't . . ."

He jumped up, went for pen and paper. "I am going to have the biggest, best, HOTTEST promotion this town has ever seen!" He lost some ground then. "Because I'm stuck with one hundred and forty-four dozen damned beads, and I am going to get unstuck."

He wrote down my dream thoughts and added some of his own. Then he decided to get the apartment group on it, and went into the hall and shouted, "Emergency!"

The clan arrived. There were all kinds of ideas: good, bad, crazy, wild, wonderful.

Mister came up with a gem. "Yust the thing—stick on boys' bikes; re . . . re . . ."

"Reflectors!" yelled Bill.

Mister was so proud he didn't have another thought, but basked in glory. "Yust the thing; little boys never get hit by cars, then. Yah, Sharlie!"

At eleven the group returned to their respective lairs, and Mac got out his portable typewriter. Big fingers flying, forehead dewy with effort, he typed the entire list.

Watching, I was overcome with love and with shame, too, for earlier suspicion . . . Miss America. I went into the bedroom and got his Christmas sweater from under the bed. After Mac put away the typewriter, I gave him the sweater.

"Katie! Terrif!" He was as tickled as a small child. "Christmas?"

"Early."

He went to the front closet. "I have something for you." He gave me a package, and when I opened it a lacy slip cascaded out. I adore lacy slips.

We beamed at each other and went to bed.

Mac spent a restless night; he mumbled about beads and twice got up to write notes.

Mr. Marcy backed Mac all the way with advertising. In the next two weeks Penneys was in the bead business. Other stores, including mine, did not have a more than usual supply. Even the public-school art departments and home-ec (shudder) sections got into the act. Mr. Hartford personally requisitioned beads, after Mac called him. Sewn or glued on velvet they were spectacular—and ranged from pictured peacocks to purses. Mac had to reorder. He was cautious, and rightfully so, it turned out, because iridescent beads were dead by Christmas.

Mac said he'd never get himself in that fix again. It's difficult in the retail business because the constant challenge is to have what the customer wants when he wants it, and in the quantity he'll buy. Even fad things such as beads. There shouldn't be, ideally, either shortages or leftovers, marked down (costs).

Oh, yes; the business world is *hard*.

Working in a store during December promotes the Christmas spirit among the personnel. The decorations are marvelous. They were especially great at Sears because there was a young kid in the display department who was a genius. He could make angels with gold spray, a bit of cloth and tinsel, and a music box inside so they sang. The people who say Christmas is too commercial may have a point, but unless a customer goes out of his head into debt, there's something wonderful about giving. I don't believe anyone forgets the meaning of Christmas, or how it began with the Baby Jesus. The Wise Men knew that giving is good for the soul. I am sure of that.

Ward AB was enjoying working on our respective gifts; the handkerchiefs were lovely. No one would imagine they had started out plain. Under supervision, I embroidered a violet or two. The men's initials (Angie was man-oriented) were bold, and the ladies' pretty. The bunnies and chicks had darling expressions. It was thrilling.

At Sears I found December customers were more courteous than usual to salespeople and to each other, though rushed. At Christmas time we all try to be good. Whenever I had a minute off, I went to the toy department and watched Santa and the children. At times I'd be so touched I'd almost cry, and on one occasion I saw Santa cry—he was a fairly tough Santa, too, smelling slightly of bourbon. It's difficult to correlate Little Adolph and his ilk with the freshly laundered (some were very raggedy-dirty and had running noses) children. They were polite, and they confided in Santy. I guess Christmas brings out the best in us, mostly. Children are great, even when they aren't. Because they believe.

Unfortunately, shoplifters look forward to Christmas as much as children. They are very active and love the crowds because it is then easier to take merchandise and wallets. We were fairly tense, watching. No one ever discovered how a chain saw disappeared, along with a snowmobile; it must have taken teamwork on the part of the thieves. One lady opened her purse to pay me, and there was a necklace in full view inside. She became absolutely white when she saw it.

"Oh, my, oh, my," she said, "that's for my grandniece. I was carrying it to the register and stopped to look at something else and dropped it in. Please accept my apologies. I would have come back . . . oh, my. . . ."

Perhaps I was a fool, but I thought she was telling the truth; something like that almost happened to me, once, but I woke up in time. Agitation like hers was hard to fake, and she was older and absent-minded.

I rang up the sale and said, "Merry Christmas!"

Mac and I had a problem about our presents. I'd buy a tie and be excited; naturally it was one I loved, and Mac enjoys a tie—it does something for him, so then I'd start thinking he should have it right away. I would get it out from under the bed—and give it to him. He did the same with me.

We couldn't help ourselves. We bought Christmas gifts, and we gave them to each other immediately. So we each had to get another, and we couldn't afford it, but we had to. We'd vow we would be strong and wait, but we would weaken every time. Neither of us had suspected we had so little character. The only things we were able to keep were Randolph's tasty plastic bone (for a week), and the almonds I blanched and browned and salted, putting them in small boxes for the apartment-house group, and for Mr. York and Mr. Clift (smallest box).

I delivered Randolph's present early. We hadn't seen him for a long time, and we were worried.

"Randolph may go in for summer friendships," said Bill. "You know the type. We're good enough to meet on the corner, warm evenings, but he doesn't want to take us home."

"Stop leering," I told Bill. "Randolph is true blue all the way."

When I got home early from work one afternoon, I decided to make a search for Randolph. Only one way to do it: knock on doors. By the time I had covered two blocks, every house, I was worn down. Everyone had met Randolph, but they didn't know his address. I would make three more tries and give up. At the very last house I heard Randolph bark. I knocked at the door and a man answered, just as I had concluded no one was home.

"What do you want?"

His bluntness surprised me. I held out the Christmas-wrapped bone. "A present for Randolph."

He smiled. "Why, that's kind of you."

"We love Randolph. He's one of the nicest people we know, but he couldn't tell us where he lived, and lately we've missed him very much."

"There is a leash law in this city, and I've been walking him. He woke all the other pooches when I let him out at 6:00 A.M. The people who called on me requesting restraint were unwilling to get up so early. Can't say I blame them."

"I'd like to see Randolph."

"Come in. I'm Jim Hamilton."

"Katie Macfarlane." I couldn't say more because Randolph hurtled into me, guided missile, and began licking my face.

"Down!" Mr. Hamilton was not permissive; he was effective. "He's alone most of the day and has too much energy; needs more exercise. I'd send him to my brother, but I like Randolph around . . . *down!*"

As a parent, Mr. Hamilton was having the usual troubles.

"Everyone likes Randolph around," I said. "Even Mr. Swensen."

"Swensen?"

"The man who owns our apartment house."

"You have landlord trouble?"

"Not really. Mr. Swensen is cross, but he doesn't mean it."

"Mine does."

"Maybe, maybe not. Ignore it."

"I'm good at that." He grinned.

"Carry on."

By this time Randolph had quieted considerably, and he

was leaning against Mr. Hamilton. They were both striking, and had the same color scheme—brown skin, expressive amber eyes. It was clear they were in tune.

"I could walk Randolph on Wednesdays and Saturdays if it would help. We miss Randolph. You can pick him up on the way home, or let us keep him overnight."

We made the deal and Jim Hamilton became one of our good friends. I had to blanch more almonds, showing no prejudice; his box was no bigger than the others (except Mr. Clift's). Randolph was a charmer; we all felt any pal of his must be worthwhile.

However, while we were talking about exercising the dog, *he* was tearing open his Christmas package. Like Mac, he enjoyed it so much, neither of us had the heart to take it away from him.

"He is a good dog," I said. "Naturally Santa will remember that."

"Naturally."

Walking Randolph, even when it was raining-sleeting, was good for me. Mac was working every night during the season, so I was glad to have company. On fair days I met all the neighbors on a new basis. The people who had accused us of being polluters were pleasant; they were frantic over the ecology and hadn't realized we were, too. The Screamer was now in nursery school, and had learned from a bright teacher that screaming would get him nowhere except out in the hall by himself. He was a handful, without doubt, but with him away part of the day his mother was making a remarkable recovery from her nervous condition.

I was lucky. At Christmas people are friendlier, as I said. I learned that Mr. Wu's second son was aping Fu Manchu, and Mrs. Wu was aloof because her Hong Kong

English was unlike ours (actually, it was better English, but not American). So I talked to her and she smiled and agreed. An ideal arrangement. There were eight children in the Wu family, which horrified the ecologists, but I pointed out to them it was too late to accomplish anything there, and anyway they were sensible, organized, intelligent, and industrious, except second son Fu.

Being a gentleman, Randolph sat patiently while I got acquainted. He was bored because he already knew the neighbors, but stared into space until I was ready to move on.

Suddenly it was Christmas week. I hadn't realized something I had anticipated so much could be that sudden.

I didn't have a present left for Mac. He didn't have one for me. We decided to make a special, special Christmas card for each other. We would put them on our tree, which we could get marked down if we waited until the last minute. It was difficult for Mac when he did his card because I was always home when he was. In order to give him time, I walked Randolph more than usual. While we walked, I composed and discarded poems in praise of Mac. Making special cards was more difficult than buying something.

We received seven invitations to parties; three we couldn't go to because they were early. We accepted the others. We couldn't stay late, but we wanted to wish everyone the merriest Christmas of all. I had pangs of envy for people not in the retail business. They seemed to have no idea that some (us) worked the day before Christmas, the day after, and mornings and nights and all the time during the holidays. Holidays? I discovered the Scrooge in me but, like Randolph, attempted to be patient with the unknowing.

There was a small problem in connection with the

parties. I was still wearing my trousseau; bought in May, there were no proper December dresses, not that I had thought about them then. Mac's wedding suit was fine, and with three new ties he felt as if everything was new. I needed something glittery. So I got out a crimson formal I'd worn in college, added some gold sequins with Mrs. Swensen's aid, and wore it with matching coat (also sequined; I could take them off in January) to the parties. Mrs. Swensen and I also pasted sequins on some dangling earrings. The effect was dramatic, although a trifle *much*, but on each occasion I'd say, "We're going *on*." I'd explained that to the hostess when I accepted each invitation, implying a highly formal occasion. It helped us to look awfully popular, and we made our entrance laughing. Since we were always late (Mac's hours), an entrance was fine. Mac didn't go for effects, and he sarcastically suggested he borrow the Penney Company Santa suit, but I promised I'd never do it again—dress like that for half an hour, and go home. It was fun, our first year.

Christmas Eve the apartment group came by on their exodus to other places and I presented the blanched almonds. I had already delivered boxes to all the neighbors I knew. They weren't much, but they were what we had. We didn't go out on the Eve because we were taking the 5:30 morning bus to the elder Macfarlanes. We'd arrive about noon and have dinner and come back the same night. The day after would be rough (and it was, what with exchanges), but it was well worth it.

Something happened that evening, though. For the best, I guess. The Swensens came by on their way to Olaf's, and Mr. Swensen was glum. He was having trouble with the disposal. He thought Mrs. Swensen had dropped a walnut in it, which she denied.

"Is it a *Kenmore* disposal?" I asked, trying to be helpful, because if it happened to be the Sears brand, I could ask a man in that department who understood Kenmore disposals backwards and forwards.

Mac flashed such a look at me I thought I'd faint.

After the Swensens left I blurted, "I've been working at Sears."

"I know."

"You do? How?"

"I saw you."

"You did?"

"I did."

"When?"

"About two months ago. Mr. Marcy asked me to go to a meeting at Greenwood Mall, and we both saw you." He grinned. "The meeting was about fad merchandise, and that was also the day they had you looking for a pants stretcher."

My face got hot; I was horribly embarrassed. There is no such thing as a pants stretcher, at least not the kind they had me search for. It's something new people have to go through; it's hazing. Eager types like me they send all around the store for a pants stretcher.

Worst, though, was Mr. Marcy knowing how ignorant I was. I was close to tears. "What did Mr. Marcy say?"

"He said, 'Dear heaven, they did that to my wife, twenty years ago.' He had no idea it was still going on, and laughed and told me Mrs. Marcy would love you forever for it."

"She worked at Sears?"

"Yes."

"*Before* or *after* they were married?"

"Both."

"Why didn't you say something?"

"You didn't want me to know," said Mac. "I tried to co-operate."

I thought I would die with love for him. "One little day, just that day . . ."

"I would have found out. Mr. Hartford mentioned you weren't teaching when I called him about the beads. To coin an expression, Katie, it's a small world."

"Oh."

"Mr. Hartford also said there would be a job for you someplace in the school system after the first of the year."

It wasn't sensible, but I got furious with Mac. "You didn't tell me? You let me suffer. . . ."

Mac had a temper, too. "Katherine, didn't you think it might be humiliating for me, not knowing? No man wants the world to be aware his wife is in some underground activity *he* hasn't been told about."

I flared. "Sears is not underground."

"Your attitude was. Why didn't you tell *me?*"

"I thought you wouldn't like it."

He sighed. "Women! You mean you don't intend to divulge anything I might not want to hear?"

"Sort of."

"No. That's not right. You're entitled to your own life, but something that affects us both has to be put on the table, Katie. You've got to understand that; if you don't— or won't—we're headed for trouble."

"I didn't want to lie," I said, miserably. "But what with the pots and pans and being a fool, and then no job . . . oh, Mac . . ."

At that moment, outside our window, the Christmas carolers started. It was the most fortunate moment of our lives. We listened to *Silent Night, Holy Night,* and *Joy to the World,* and *We Three Kings of Orient Are.*

163

We had time to think.

Mac went out and thanked the carolers, and I watched him give the leader a dollar, our coffee-and-toast money for the bus trip. He came back.

"Probably," I said, going to him and putting my arms around him, "the bus won't stop long enough for us to have breakfast. I'll make sandwiches."

"Ah, Katie . . . Katie . . ."

"I am sorry, Mac. Sorry."

He held me, and we heard the carol from down the street—*It Came Upon a Midnight Clear*.

Mac carried me in to the big chair, and I sat on his lap, my head on his shoulder.

In a small voice, after a while, I said, "I wonder about Mr. Hartford."

"You like working at Sears?"

"Yes. I've learned so much about how it is with you, and I'm grateful. And I like all the bosses, and the people. Sears is a good company."

"True . . . you always wanted to teach, Katie."

"I still do. It's the children, Mac. I love them, even the naughty ones. Maybe *especially* the naughty ones."

"Then you must teach, and you are trained to do it. Give Sears proper notice and finish with honor."

"Yes, but suppose Mr. Hartford changes his mind? You know Mr. Clift. . . ."

"You can't play the angles, Katie. Sometimes you have to take a chance. You'll have to trust to luck and Mr. Hartford. You can't let Sears down and quit without giving them a chance to replace you."

I murmured. "I suppose not."

"No."

"Other people do."

"You want to be like those people?"

"I'd want to, Mac, if a teaching job were offered; I mean, I *might*, if it came to this or that."

He patted my head.

" 'This or that' is simple for you," I said. "You're natural."

"It isn't simple. I won't tell Mr. Marcy about the unlocked door until I *retire*. I'm no paragon."

Mac had humbled himself by recalling the unlocked door. He did it for me, and it wasn't good for him. I thought a prayer, then, of thanks, and also promised I'd not request humbleness from him in the future. A little might be good, but not much. Mac needed to be sure. And he wasn't sure he'd tell Mr. Marcy someday, because neither of us would ever be old, or retire.

The bus trip to the Macfarlanes' place in the country seemed interminable the next morning. We had left the M.G. in the parking lot at the bus station; its engine was not well and Mac hadn't had time to doctor it. It was a good thing I had packed the gifts (handkerchiefs) in my old cardboard suitcase, along with almonds and a superior Penney Company fruitcake. I never would have remembered the things I wanted to take—stumbling around the apartment before dawn. The bus went on and on and on, and there wasn't ever a stop long enough for coffee and toast, so it was as well Mac had given our dollar.

We spent a lovely afternoon; the turkey was perfect (both smell and taste) and the bayberry candles flickered and the huge tree from the Macfarlane acres, with the antiquated trimming, was the most beautiful we had seen. I've heard it isn't fashionable to love your mother-in-law, but I loved Mrs. Macfarlane. If I could be a combination of our two mothers, I . . . well, I guess I'd be too good; moreover, I might develop a split personality; Bill, the psychiatrist-to-be, was forever worrying about splits. Still, if I became a little like each of them, it would be fine.

Stuffed with food and Christmas joy, we took the bus back to the city. (Workday tomorrow.) The cardboard suitcase, a bit soggy, held leftover turkey and dressing, as well as presents we'd opened. Mrs. Macfarlane had made an entire afghan for me, shaded rose and gray; Mr. Macfarlane had carved an intricate and lovely crèche. We knew we had been given future heirlooms, and our presents were paltry, though the senior Macfarlanes did not think so, and they said our efforts and our presence were the greatest gifts of all. I knew the time would soon come when I could call them "Mother" and "Father" and mean it.

The bus was packed with weary celebrators, but one traveler made the journey fascinating. There was nothing sad or sentimental about him; yet he managed to make us all realize we were lucky. He had been on the bus when we boarded it, and he said loudly he'd come straight through that day from the big range. Apparently, he had been saying this for some time, adding, too, that he didn't know where he was going, but he was glad he had left. To me, there was something terrible about traveling all of Christmas Day from the big range to nowhere. He was a cowboy, a proper one—from high-heeled, silver-inlaid boots to jeans and shirt, fringed Indian vest, and rough brown leather coat. His hat was ten gallon, the wide brim tenderly rolled upwards. His gloves were gauntlets that were fashioned for a firm grip on the rein. His face was crisscrossed with seams earned from a lifetime of summer heat and winter winds laced with rain and snow.

I didn't know his name, but I recognized him because I had grown up in ranching country. He would have only one name, like Slats or Tiny or Chub—none of which described him, and were given to him for that reason. He was The Stranger. He drifted from one spread to another, from one foreman to another, one cookhouse to another, and another. Every bunk was his, and none belonged to him. A good man; honest, hard-working, capable. Alone, by chance or by choice, but always alone; withdrawn from the group around the campfire, sitting on the stool at the end of the bar. Apart: listening to the sound of others, waiting for a need—for what, to what—that no one knew. A gentle man who had lived so roughly, he retreated from the world and himself.

As long as the bus was moving, he slept. But when we paused—and there were many brief stops to let a passenger off, take on another, or to drop off or pick up packages, rope tied, and cartons—The Stranger would stand.

Swaying, he made an announcement that never varied. "I find this very *trying*." His soft voice edged with harshness, he peered ahead—down the lonely road.

When the bus started again he would fall back and sleep.

At every crossroad, railway track, and town, he stood and spoke his piece. "I find this very *trying*."

He said it at Timberlane and Bear Creek and Ketchatoo and Adeline and Durbin . . . at Jones Lake and Oneato and Yakitan . . . at Kimberly and Hilard . . . everywhere.

"*I find this very trying.*"

Not for him the oaths of the common man, the obscenity of the in groups, the imprecation of the imaginative.

"*I find this very trying.*"

We laughed at first, and at the last we laughed. I am sure, later, we remembered.

I would always remember.

Where was the big range? Where had he been?
The Stranger.
Where was he going?
Where?

The M.G. wouldn't start when we arrived at the parking lot in a heavy rainstorm. I shivered in the car, and Mac worked frantically with the ailing engine. It was a long time before it coughed and lived, died, then lived again. The M.G. suffered asthmatic attacks all the way home. I was frozen; Mac was cold, as well as soaking wet, but he wasn't sneezing. I was, violently.

We were also *tired* when we went into the apartment. The Day was nearly over. There were only minutes left of our first Christmas together. Enough.

I opened Mac's card. There was a little tree, a tiny star above it. And it said,

> I only know
> I love you.

All in iridescent beads.

On Mac's card I had drawn a tie tack, complete with pearl and poem:

> If I had
> A magic wand
> Everything
> Would be
> For you.

Mac said my card was best.
I said his was.

8

The morning after Christmas when the alarm rang, I sat up. This was routine. When I sat up, Mac got out of bed, and I could snuggle down for a few minutes more. Mac didn't mind, because he had the bathroom to himself and could move slowly until he was accustomed to (1) bright light and (2) the world.

For me, that morning, the world was odd; the walls went in and out and the furniture whirled, including the bed. I groaned and collapsed.

Mac, standing in the doorway, surveyed me. "You have a cold."

"I hab sombthing buch worse than a code," I said.

And I did. I was smitten by a foul bug that left me helpless. Mac notified Mrs. Swensen before he left for work. He was disgustingly healthy after his ice-cold, soggy experience with the stalled M.G. I resented it.

Mrs. Swensen brought tea and toast, and I ungratefully could not eat, but was later able to try again with better results. Bill Shaw came to check and said I should have plenty of liquids, aspirin, and bed rest. I thought briefly about Ward AB and Sears and passed those duties off on my subconscious. I felt too dreadful to surface.

Time went on and I was suspended in it, a mass of misery. Mentally as well as physically, I was not myself at all. I concentrated on surviving in Bunyan's Slough of Despond.

Bill advised Mac to sleep on the davenport. I couldn't decide whether Mac was anxious for me to get well fast because the davenport was uncomfortable (lumpy; too short—he had to curl up and his knees were in a draft), or because he cared. I, frankly, did not care about anything, and doubted I ever would again. I gave fleeting consideration to people who never have good health, and asked Bill eventually if my complication might be terminal. After all, three days had gone by and I was still supine.

Bill laughed. "Katie, you have what our parents call influenza and I call a virus. Whatever it is, you'll get better despite yourself. I never imagined I'd see you give up."

He made me furious. *He* wasn't ill. I glared from my red-rimmed eyes (I had checked them; sure enough), sneezed, and said, "Go away."

He repeated, cheerily, to keep on with liquids. *I* knew I needed some miracle drug, but he left before I could give him the word. No one has any patience with a person who is not performing. I wanted my mother, and she wasn't there. I couldn't mention it because I was supposed to be an adult.

One morning I got up and examined my tongue at the mirror. It appeared almost normal, whatever that was. The walls stayed in place, too. As I crept back into the unmade bed, I was heartened, though weak. I'd get over the bug.

The following evening I was wearing a housecoat when

Mac came home, and had managed a light dinner. Mary and Sue had shopped for groceries; all Mac could cook was canned soup.

My cough persisted for about two weeks, even after I went back to Sears to give notice and finish out my time, with honor. Mr. Hartford, the assistant school superintendent, called after January 1, as he promised. He understood about the flu and Sears, and said there was a place for me, roving sub, when I was strong enough.

I'd not celebrated New Year's, and Mac was forced to cancel three parties. I almost got sick again, thinking of them.

"You can't stand to miss a thing, can you, Katie?" Mac asked, when I was in fighting trim again.

"No." I was fierce. "It was almost worth it, though, to call all our friends on New Year's Day, early." I grinned wickedly; most of them had felt worse than I did. It was great.

Mac shook his head. "A mean streak there."

"Yar. When I cry because I can't go out, I expect others to suffer with me."

It was ironical that my last paycheck from Sears was stolen. That is, it was stolen after I had cashed the check. One minute I had money, and was thinking of buying some clearance items, and then when I looked, the wallet was gone. I told Mr. Folger and Mr. York and everyone else about it. They were genuinely sorry, but sympathy does not take place of funds. There was nothing for me to do but go home on the bus, paying with some of the currency the unprintable thief had left in my coin purse. Usually hard currency is not stolen; it jingles. It was sad I didn't have many coins.

My fury was short lived because in our mailbox was a

check for twenty-five dollars. I had won a newspaper prize on "How to Make a Dollar Go Farther."

I have a tendency to mourn over past errors, and despite the prize, I yearned for the stolen paycheck, although my grief was somewhat assuaged. I don't know what I would have done if I hadn't entered the newspaper contest. Receiving the good news when I was about to go into a decline was a coincidence too good to be true. It happened, though.

When I told Mac about the loss he said, predictably, "Forget it! It's *done*."

He always said that, and he didn't remind me that he had told me and *told* me to put my wallet in the zippered part of my purse. That usually prevents sneaky fingers, although not always.

There was a small comfort in the knowledge my handbag was intact plus identification cards. I had seen shoppers astonished when they discovered they were grasping only the handles of the purse, the straps having been cut with a razor. Anything can happen in a crowd, shopping, with jerks present, as they always seem to be.

Mac wasn't happy with beans for dinner three weeks straight. I served so many bean variations, he started keeping track of the recipes. "Let me count the ways," he murmured, as did Elizabeth Barrett Browning, but not about beans.

Roving substitute was wonderful with the exception of one small episode. Mac says I should always plan on *one*, but I don't.

When I went to see Mr. Hartford, there were other people being interviewed, so I sat in a corner in one of those office chairs with the spring back. I couldn't know it had been placed there for the janitor to take away and repair. How could I, in all fairness, know? I waited, blissfully. There was a shaft of sun shining in my eyes, and it was warm and cozy, and I leaned back.

Whammo! The chair didn't turn over, it dipped inexorably, and there I was, in a sort of yoga position, scrambling to hold my skirt down (or up; however you look at it). It was undignified, but I will say it's the first time I ever came near to standing on my head successfully; always before I had crumpled in the middle. In the chaos that followed—Mr. Hartford and three others tried for some time to get me and the chair upright—I was grateful I had on the lacy slip Mac had given me for Christmas. He always comes through, even when he isn't *there*.

Mr. Hartford apologized, smothering laughter, and presently he gave way and laughed and laughed. Everyone joined in, including me. Perhaps it was a good beginning, after all. Especially with the slip; probably the viewers would carry an image of me wearing lovely underclothes. That isn't a bad image to have. I didn't have any other gorgeous slips, but it is nice to think about.

The children . . .

Oh, the children in school. They say the most perceptive things and ask the shrewdest questions in the world. Such as: "Did your eyelashes grow like that, or do you put them on, nervously—QUIET!—the way Mommy does?"

I didn't become acquainted with individuals as well as I would have liked because I left classes as soon as the regular teachers were able to return. Almost always illness —theirs or their family's—was responsible for a teacher's absence. They were a dedicated lot; they came back as soon as possible, often before they felt truly well. It's best to have full strength when dealing with little ones; they take it all.

—————

173

Working only three days a week, I found I had time on my hands. I had given up on the baseboards permanently. I could then consider my novel. It would be about the retail business, I decided, with emphasis on Penneys and Sears. Surely there would be a lot of people interested, because the retail business is the biggest one in the world. Practically no one realizes it.

It was difficult starting the novel, however. There was always something I would rather do. I guess I'd rather live than write about it. I had a serious block.

One Saturday morning as I was staring at a piece of paper—not entirely blank because I had written on it, "Six Nights a Week: Chapter 1"—the phone rang. My friends knew I did not like the muse or whatever (nothing had happened as yet) interrupted on Sat. mornings, so I knew the call was important.

"Katie . . . Katie?"

I had to come back from contemplation of Chapter 1, so I suppose I seemed not *present*. "Yar."

"It's Mac."

"I love you."

"I do you, too. Look, Bill Phillips, the New York Penney man, is coming to dinner tonight."

"Oh."

"We are not having beans, I hope."

"No beans," I said, stupidly. "Baked stuffed pork chops."

"Fine! You have enough?"

"What?"

"Pork chops."

"Certainly. I am going to the store for them right now." I was relieved I did not have to think more about Chapter 1. "Is anyone else coming with Mr. Phillips?"

"No." He hung up suddenly, forgetting to say good-by. I knew he was intent on making a sale.

Forthwith, I went into action; I had an errand of my own scheduled. Time was running short. Went about my business, then down the street where Randolph was waiting for his walk. He was so smart he always realized what day it was, which is more than I do. I went to his house, dug the key out of a flowerpot—Jim Hamilton said a sensible burglar would look there immediately, but we changed pots occasionally to make it more difficult—and with Randolph on leash, went to the market.

There was only one person Randolph hated, and he was shopping, so we took longer than usual. Randolph and I had to lurk outside the store until the man left. Funny, meeting the guy he came off holy, but I trusted Randolph's instinct and agreed no one could be that holy and mean it. Randolph was intent on biting him and once tore the seat of his trousers; the language we heard was worse than Slem's, so the joker could not have spent as much time in church as he pretended. It was all very embarrassing. A standard French poodle has big teeth. One time, Randolph had attempted to box with the guy, standing on his hind legs and cuffing. It was hilarious, because the dog resembled Wild Willie Slovak, the fighter; Randolph was also two feet taller than his involuntary opponent. We were in a hurry today, so we lurked instead of getting involved in a nonsensical situation.

When I was shopping, at last, I began wondering if Mac had invited more than one guest. I mean, he was casual about invitations. I was tempted to phone Penneys and make sure, but I knew how retail men hate being called while working—the boss frowns upon it, too—so I refrained. Also, it would be better to spend the ten cents telephone charge on the groceries. As usual, I was close to being flat broke.

I decided to serve broiled grapefruit for the first course;

it would be festive with brown-sugar glaze and a maraschino cherry in the center picking up the color of the red (leftover Christmas) candles. One is supposed to think about these things, according to the articles in the ladies' magazines about smart women. There was a small, rather droopy poinsettia—late bloomer, I suppose; missed the holidays—so I got that for the table and bought three specially cut, thick pork chops, broccoli, and salad stuff. Penneys fruitcake, steamed, with whipped topping under pressure, would be the dessert. I had a can I'd been saving for an important occasion. This was it.

Randolph and I trudged home. He was so courteous he gave up his favorite sniffing tree, because he had studied me with gleaming, knowledgeable, amber eyes and had concluded this was a workday; no fun. I saw him decide it. Randolph was, above all, considerate.

I had unloaded the groceries on the kitchen counter, which is always depressing because I have to put everything away in a proper manner; for example, celery. Mac thought celery came in curls, and radishes turned into roses all by themselves. Not so. One must wash and curl and/or cut, and use ice water to accomplish it. I was glad Mac was the way he was, because I'd seen husbands take over the kitchen with the greatest-chefs-are-men bit, and then the wife had a hard row to hoe proving she earned her keep. A woman always has to prove that; women's lib is no help.

The phone rang.

"Katie?" Mac, again.

"Speaking."

"You have the chops?"

"Yep."

"Three?"

"Yar." Oh, dear . . .

"Katie, there are two men coming. Bill Phillips and Steve Lamb; he's in draperies."

I wished he'd stay there.

But I heard a note of desperation in Mac's voice, and I said, offhandedly, "Can do. Will split chops."

"You're wonderful, Katie."

It seemed Mac loved me most when we were talking about food or having people to dinner.

I went to the Swensens, and they both came to our apartment; Mr. Swensen with a hack saw. He divided those thick chops like a pro. We now had six, and I would make a lot of dressing, and would cook them all tonight. Impressive, and no bother with the little stuffing pockets. I was safe on the grapefruit, since they had cost four for ninety-six cents. I put the four in our sunny window, where the sun would make them sweeter. Maybe.

It had been a close call. I leaned against the counter.

"Don't these men have *homes?*" I asked.

"They're traveling," said Mrs. Swensen. "Mister used to be on the road."

I sighed. "If a Penney buyer ever invited us out to dinner, he would have a friend in me forever. I suppose wives don't count."

Mister spoke up, unexpectedly. "Men're yust lonely for lady cooking. Yah, Sharlie. On-the-road eatin's not so goot."

I got to work. I even sang as I made the dressing and curled the celery and cleaned broccoli, which I would cook at the last minute. Mac hates to come into the apartment when there is a smell such as boiling broccoli or cabbage or fish. After he's in, it's all right.

I hung up my best guest towels and gave the baseboards a fast swipe. The fact was, despite a strong desire to go out for dinner, I liked Penney buyers. They were good types. Even the garment manufacturers thought so. Whuff told us once that his uncle in New York (the Campagnas had relatives everywhere) was a dress manufacturer, and he said Penney buyers were tough but fair and never treated him like an animal. Even if the New York garment center is a jungle, and some say it is, no one can stand to be regarded as less than human.

By six I was ready and waiting. The transistor was on low, good music, my ruffled apron (a gift from Ward AB) folded on top of the refrig, also ready. The M.G. snorted into its stall, and I watched three large men get out. It was wonderful what they were willing to go through to have a home-cooked meal. Driving, Mac must have been lost in a maze of arms and legs. When there are more than two in the M.G., one has a tendency to develop octopus syndrome.

Mac remembered to bring the guests around to the front door instead of coming through the kitchen. When I was introduced, I found Steve Lamb as easy to meet as Bill Phillips was the time before. Bill looked reflectively at the draperies—Penney men have a tendency to notice fabrics. When he had been at the apartment with Mr. Marcy, I'd borrowed Mary's, and he probably recalled they were different, but he didn't say a word. I didn't volunteer any information.

Usually I serve nonalcoholic hot spiced grape juice with a marshmallow or two floating on top as dinner appetizer. I'd forgotten the grape juice.

When we were sitting in the living room (I had a floor cushion), I said, "Do you like aquavit?"

"I've heard of it," said Bill. "Never had any."

"What is it?" asked Steve.

I explained about Olaf's gift. The guests decided to try aquavit. While Mac was getting out the ice, I ran to Swensens, borrowed a chair, and got instructions on serving the Norwegian drink.

"Yust a little," said Mr. Swensen.

When I got back, Mac had found the tumblers, and not wishing to look cheap, he'd poured more than a little, plus adding a twist of lemon to give interest. It was too late to do anything about the size of the serving; Mac had already started into the living room with the tray. He didn't like wifely advice in his department, anyway.

I think about that evening—something I try to avoid— and realize that was the moment when the dinner party started to fall apart.

The drink didn't have much taste, and we decided to have another. We mixed the aquavit with ginger ale; it was better. Actually, one would never guess there was anything in the glass but ginger ale; in fact, I had *only* ginger ale in my *third* drink.

Randolph, temporarily tied in the hall, emitted a sharp bark, so I brought him to the party. He solemnly offered a paw handshake, and we were as proud of him as if he had been our own.

After the introductions, Randolph went into the dinette and settled under the table, out of the way. In the kitchen, I put the broccoli on to cook and prepared the grapefruit— the actual glazing would take only a few minutes.

I went back into the living room, and Steve got a floor pillow and sat beside me. At my request, he brought out pictures of his wife and three little boys; a handsome family. We visited, and I came to the conclusion New Yorkers were almost like anyone else.

"Aquavit," said Bill Phillips suddenly, "has authority."

179

He smiled. We did, too.

I was about to get up to put the grapefruit under the broiler when Randolph came to see us. He was acting furtive; unlike himself. He walked carefully to the middle of the room and, sides heaving, began to regurgitate grapefruit. Perhaps more time had passed than I realized; I'd lost track of Randolph and had no idea he was in the kitchen. Acquavit stretches time. In my presence, Randolph had never so much as looked at the counter, even when I had hamburger defrosting, so it was a surprise to find he had devoured the first course.

We were all amazed and paralyzed. It took Mac a while to get into action and Randolph's grapefruit loomed high on the rug.

"That dog has more talent and capacity than I would have thought possible," said Steve.

Mac grabbed Randolph and took him to the basement to recover on an old comforter we kept near the furnace for him. I got a plastic bag and delicately removed the debris. Under the circumstances we conducted ourselves very well, unprepared as we were for such an emergency.

No one felt up to eating dinner right then, so Mac fixed a tiny bit more of the aquavit and everyone downed it quickly. The Norwegians, we agreed, are a remarkable people, and we were grateful to Olaf. I don't believe we could have overlooked Randolph's *faux pas* with the aid of simple grape juice. Even so, next day, I swore that no more of Mr. Swensen's favorite drink would pass through our doorway.

The pork chops were nicely browned, the broccoli sufficiently cooked. Somehow everyone got into the act. Steve wore my fancy apron and tossed the salad, while Bill stirred the hollandaise sauce. He realized it had to be stirred continuously; splashed only a little on his own coat. Mac lit the candles and poured the water. We sat at the table and the men talked business. It was fun, and instructive, too. We heard Randolph howling once or twice, but ignored him. We didn't want to think about him at all. It was the only time I've ever been anything but sympathetic toward Randolph. Like the rest of us, he could be forgiven his frailties, but not now.

It was a clear February evening, with a sky full of stars; brisk and beautiful. I suggested we take a walk before the dessert. We would deliver Randolph to his house, and the walk would do us good. It did. We came back in fine fettle —I think we were still feeling the effects of the aquavit, and anticipated the fruitcake, which I had left steaming.

I don't believe I have mentioned the apartment house bear traps. Often, when one couple went out, the other two couples in the group built a bear trap to welcome them, as well as to inform the stay-at-homes as to time of return. With our keys unlocking all doors, there was no problem in getting into any apartment. Our bear traps (Whuff's idea) were made by piling canned goods and other articles such as pans and kitchen utensils so precariously that the whole works fell over with thunderous consequences the moment the door was opened. If the entrants weren't cautious, there was a possibility of a slightly smashed toe (Whuff was used to injuries in line of duty: football), but nothing serious. The Swensens did not approve, but were willing to give a little leeway to youth and high spirts. It took skill to build a proper bear trap, and it was Whuff's specialty, though Mac was no slouch, once he got the idea.

I guess the Shaws and the Campagnas thought our guests had gone home. When we came back we weren't as careful as usual (the aquavit). When Mac flung open the door, the trap was sprung. Steve Lamb and Bill Phillips were totally unprepared, and they reacted. They both hopped around, swearing; Steve louder than Bill.

I said, with admiration, it was Romeo's finest effort, and that took some explaining. Steve and Bill were enough older so the generation gap showed. However, they were almost as fascinated by Romeo's name as they were by the trap. Bill said he knew a Romeo Campagna, garment manufacturer, in New York, who was infinitely ingenious. Sounded like the same family.

The fruitcake had steamed nicely and resembled a pudding. We all used the floor cushions; we'd long since given up formality. I had not put the whipped topping on in case anyone preferred their dessert plain. It would have been better if I had taken care of the topping in the kitchen; everyone did want it, and as I was adding it to Mac's cake, he said something amusing and I laughed, missed my aim, and got a mound of whipped cream on his favorite tie. It would come off with cleaning fluid, I assured him.

Steve said if I'd scored a higher hit, Mac would have looked like Santa.

Because we were sitting on the floor, what happened next was more effective than it would have been otherwise. There was an explosion from the nether regions immediately beneath us. Bill, Steve, Mac, and I were immobile.

The first explosion was followed by about sixteen more. Silence, then.

"My God," said Steve, "what's that?"

"Some kind of an invasion," yelled Bill Phillips. "Man the ramparts!" He meant it.

There was another explosion.

Steve put his dessert dish on the floor beside him. As he got up there was another blast, and Steve stepped in the dessert, but stubbornly hopped to the front door.

He hesitated to open it. "They make bear traps outside, too?" he asked. He wasn't a coward, but he had reached a point where he couldn't stand one more thing. Not one more.

"No," I said.

Mac was on his feet. "Listen, guys . . ."

"My mother always told me *never* to go west of the Alleghenies. I sure as hell wish I had listened to her," said Steve.

"Listen, guys," said Mac, sort of pleading. "It's the *wine*."

We heard the Shaws and Campagnas and Swensens running down the basement stairs.

Steve and Bill were fascinated as Mac and I explained about the wine we had put away to age. I was tired of explaining all the time, but it had been that kind of evening.

"You may have invented something," said Bill with Eastern aplomb. "The stuff seems to have more power than a Molotov cocktail."

"If you don't mind," I said, stiffly, "I'd prefer not to hear the word."

"Molotov?"—bewildered.

"Cocktail," I said. "It is alcohol that is the root of all evil, not money."

Bill explained what a Molotov cocktail was.

In the hall we heard Mr. Swensen. "Yah, Sharlie!"

"Who's *that*?"—Steve.

We told him.

Someone knocked on the front door. It was Whuff. "Reporting, sir." He saluted Mac smartly.

"Yes, Sergeant?" Mac was calm.

"Uh . . . well, there is no wine left. . . ."

BAM!

"*Now* there is no wine left."

The four of us listened.

"And there are more damned grapes stuck all over the damned basement—on the ceiling, on the walls—than there are in the entire state of California."

"My God," said Steve. "A purple cellar. My God." He seemed to be in a rut, swearing. On the other hand, he may have been praying. He sounded deadly serious.

"Mac . . ."—Whuff.

"Yes, Romeo . . ."

"The Mister says we can clean it up tonight and tomorrow."

"*Now?*"

" 'S all right, brother. Enjoy your company. We'll take it in shifts. You can be on the second shift."

Mac slumped, then stood straight. "Okay."

Standing behind Whuff in the hall were Sue, and Mary and Bill Shaw. We invited them in, and I served plain fruitcake (no topping) to the group. The evening had left me with a severe loss of confidence.

Bill Phillips and Steve Lamb listened clinically, I thought, to the rest of our story of the attempt to make wine.

The Penney guests announced they must leave. Mac offered to drive them downtown in the M.G., but they didn't want us to go to any more trouble, they said. They called a taxi, and when they left Steve kissed my hand and said he would never forget all this, and Bill gallantly seconded him.

I felt certain they would not forget.

Whuff went down to the basement, and Mac said, "I have a headache and I've got to get to bed in order to be ready for the next shift." He was sitting on the davenport, so benumbed he hadn't noticed he was on the biggest lump. "I'll be famous in the Penney Company," he predicted gloomily. "I don't suppose anything more can happen."

BAM!

Period.

Mac started laughing, and so did I.

Presently he said, "There are no more surprises left for me in the world."

I wasn't sure about that.

He closed his eyes, leaned back against the davenport. "Are you all right?"

"I guess so." He continued to rest his eyes. "I think I'll grow a beard."

"Uh. It will be flaming red."

"Naturally."

"You don't like beards."

"I need a change."

"You have to trim them."

He grunted.

"Beards itch."

"That'll be my reward." He spoke with the deceptive gentleness that meant he wanted to hit something or someone. "When it itches I can scratch it."

I knew how it was. I was sympathetic.

But life is full of surprises; you have to roll with the punches. Mac shouldn't become fatly complacent, at his age.

I had vowed never to keep another secret from him. So I whispered, "The doctor said today I was pregnant."

He sat straight; stared.

"We are going to have a baby."

Mac went *slumf-sssssssss* . . .

I have always believed he fainted. He denies it.

He was relaxing, he says. And gathering strength for the future.